Rock Hard

Love Hard

Rock Hard Musical #1

For age 18 and up.

kailin gow

Rock Hard Love Hard (Rock Hard Musical #1)

Rock Hard Love Hard (Rock Hard Musical #1)
Published by THE EDGE
THE EDGE is an imprint of Sparklesoup Inc.
Copyright © 2014 Kailin Gow

For information, please contact:
THE EDGE at Sparklesoup
14252 Culver Dr., A732
Irvine, CA 92604
www.theEDGEbooks.com
First Edition.
ISBN: 978-1-59748-103-8

Kailin Gow

DEDICATION

To my drama teachers and professors in college who instilled a love for the stage, for discipline, and for teamwork in me. Bet you never saw this one coming...

PROLOGUE

The lights were so bright as I looked up into them, knowing that the ball was heading my way. It was up to me to get it done. All I had to do was catch the pig skin and run a few yards into the end zone and we'd win our division. I'd done it often enough before and it was time to show my stuff again.

Focus, I thought. Then I caught the ball and began to run toward the end zone. I could hear the USC fans shouting and cheering me on and I was going full speed ahead. Then it happened. Something with the force of a tornado tossing a semi came across my left side, smashed into me, and sent me flying backward into the ground.

I had no idea what was happening until I felt the heavy impact of a defensive lineman on top of me, crushing me into the ground. It hurt so damn bad and my body wasn't in a natural position. My legs were straight ahead of me and even with the banging of helmets and clash of padding smashing into each other, I heard a snap. It echoed through my body and was followed by a rip that travelled up my entire spine and sent me into pain unlike I'd ever experienced before.

"Get off, get off," I heard a ref shouting. Everyone cleared off of me and I couldn't see straight. I was in so much pain and I thought I was going to puke all over the damn field. I couldn't even get my hand up to my mouth to pull out my mouth guard so I could breathe better.

Then I heard the sounds that confirmed my fear. There were gasps from the players who were standing around me, as well as from the bleachers of the stadium.

People started asking me questions and I couldn't focus. Finally the coach was kneeling down by me and telling everyone else to back up.

Rock Hard Love Hard (Rock Hard Musical #1)

"Can you move at all?" he asked me.

I tried to move and realized I couldn't. My mind was willing me to move, but my entire body felt numb and I couldn't get it to do what I wanted. I began trembling instantly, shaking and sweating, as if I was standing in 100° weather. "I can't move. I can't move."

Am I paralyzed? I don't understand.

"We need the medics. Call an ambulance," the coach shouted. "Everyone that doesn't need to be here get the hell out of here."

My teammates and the opposing team took some steps back and knelt down. I saw the face of the one guy from Utah, who we were playing. He looked horrified and shaken. I could see him mouth to me that he was sorry. I tried to nod, but had no idea whether I actually did it or not.

Medics began swarming around me, asking me many questions and trying to get me on a flat board so they could lift me up onto the stretcher that was now on the field. What happened next, I can't say for certain, but when I woke up I was at the hospital and there were people looking over me.

"Hayworth, can you understand me?" a nurse asked.

I nodded my head.

"The doctor's on his way."

I just stared at her and the look on her face was very cautious and guarded. I immediately remembered thinking I might be paralyzed and wondered if it was true and that's why she was looking at me that way. I stared down at my feet and could barely see them from the flat position I was in. Then I began to will myself to lift my leg up.

"No, no. Don't move Hayworth. Don't move," the nurse said.

"I need to know that I can," I said. My voice didn't even sound like mine. It sounded like the voice of a scared child, not a twenty year old wide receiver for a college dynasty.

"Hayworth, this is Dr. Jamison. I need you to remain relaxed."

"What's wrong with me?" I asked.

"You've broken your hip and tore some of the connecting ligaments around it."

"Do I need surgery?"

"Yes, we'll need to pin and plate the fracture spots so they grow back properly. It's a fairly common procedure, but you'll be out for the rest of the season, son."

"That's impossible. My scholarship," I said. Sure, I obviously loved football, but I also loved going to college. According to my mother, the real bread and butter in my life would come from a good education more so than football. That was a means to an end. Only, the end couldn't happen until I graduated.

"I'm sure that something will be worked out with that," the doctor said. "For now, we have to get you into surgery. The sooner the better."

An anesthesiologist came up to me and put a mask over my face. "Count backwards from 10 to 1, Hay. This won't take long."

"10, 9, 8, 7, 6, 5...."

The next thing I knew I was awake again. I looked around, trying to focus on everything happening around me. I finally saw a maroon sweater. It was the coach and he was staring at me, but not really paying attention.

"Hey coach," I whispered. My mouth was so dry that I couldn't get anything out more than those croaky words.

"Glad you're awake, Hay. How you doing?"

"They said I can't play the rest of the season, but that's not an option. I can't lose my scholarship. I have to play to keep it."

"Don't worry about that right now. We'll see how you're doing in a week or two."

"Am I on IR?"

"Temporarily, yes. So that shouldn't impact anything."

"And if I have to go to permanent IR for the season?"

"Let's worry about that *if* that time comes, Hay."

I nodded, not sure what to say about it. I knew the coach was right and it was best for the team, but I was thinking about what was best for me. Losing my football scholarship wasn't best for me.

"I called your parents. They want you to call when you're up to it. I've been keeping them informed though."

"Thanks," I said. I knew my parents couldn't come out to see me, even with this situation, and it just made the moment sting a bit more.

All I could do was count on the coach's words to be my inspiration, but unfortunately two weeks came and I was still in so much pain, not able to walk without getting exhausted and feeling jolts of pain shoot through my entire body. My mood had gone dour and life seemed pretty hopeless. I just couldn't lose that scholarship or else I'd be royally screwed. My parents didn't have the money because they'd just had to close their restaurant down, draining every last resource before doing that.

Coach had still had me on IR after two weeks and I was psyched, thinking that maybe I'd be able to get back into the game within the next two weeks. Finally, four weeks since the accident had passed and I didn't get the pains any longer and could go on the treadmill at a steady pace for an hour. It was big progress.

There was a knock on my apartment door and I walked over to answer it. I looked through the peep hole and saw the coach standing there. I had no idea what he wanted, or so I told myself.

"Hey there, got a minute."

"Too many minutes," I said, laughing. However, I sensed my day of reckoning was coming and I really wasn't ready to hear it. My failure to accept the inevitable had led me to a false sense of security.

"Look, I've been doing some thinking and researching."

"And..."

"I can't keep you on the team, Hay. It's just not possible and they're starting to chew my ass off about having you on temp IR."

I put my head down into my hands. What was I going to do?

"However, I found out about a scholarship available at USC that might allow you to stay here for academics."

"Really? What is it?" That was the most hope I'd felt in weeks.

"It's for the music department, tied to some fancy off-Broadway production they're doing here. Some bigwig is coming in to work with it. In short, his father had gone to USC and loved the arts. He started a scholarship program because of it."

"Music? Me? I'm in school for architecture." My hope turned into a lead balloon.

"Well, from, what the guys say, you're like Pavarotti in the showers. You just have to bring it to the stage."

"I did a little singing in high school and was okay at it. It got tossed to the side for football."

"Well, I'd consider bringing it back if I were you. It may not be ideal, Hay, but it's a solution."

"Okay, got it, coach. Thanks for the lead. I'll give it a try."

Coach left and I made my way to the bathroom to stare at myself in the mirror. My blonde hair had grown out a bit and was wild looking. I shook my head, staring into my blue eyes and questioned my sanity and desperation. Could I be in a musical again? Could I even fit in with the theater crowd? I had no idea, but if it was my best chance I was going to take it. Then I reached over and ate a chocolate chip cookie that some girl, who wanted to make her move on me while I was less mobile, made for me. Even almost paralyzed, girls took notice of me. Normally I would shrug it off, maybe go out with one or two of them sometime and if I was in the mood, spend the night with them. No big deal, just having fun with them and nothing else. But this time, now that it wasn't so much as how far I could throw or how fast I could run, maybe it was a good thing that people found me attractive…maybe it would help me land the role for the musical and get my scholarship to stay in college.

Not bad, I thought. The cookie tasted much better. Then I finished it and went over to my computer to find out everything I could about this musical.

CHAPTER 1

Another two weeks had passed and I found myself walking into the theater at USC. I made my way to the table where I checked in for auditions and was prepared to go through with this madness. I'd give it my all because my life literally depended on it, but I didn't feel all that confident that I was cut out for this type of thing. My reputation for profound words and prose mostly stemmed from the invitations I extended to the females that seemed to always follow me around.

I was greeted by three pairs of scrutinizing eyes, all looking me over as if I was auditioning for the most coveted role in the world. There were two guys, one very polished and charismatic looking, the other was a bit more casual and had a bald head that reflected the overhead lighting of the theater upon it. And then there was a woman. She wasn't just any woman though. She was full out smoking hot. She had long straight dark hair, large smoky exotic eyes that made me think about what it would be like to look into those eyes as I was sliding into her, and high cheek bones which were accentuated by full lips and luscious curves. She was unlike any woman I'd seen in a long time. She didn't have to work to sell the look. It was just there and I just wanted to take advantage of it.

"So, who do we have here?" The bald man asked me that question and had a smirk on his face. Apparently I hadn't hid my appreciation for the beauty next to him all that well.

"Hayworth James," I said. "I'm here to audition for the musical."

"So I see," he said. Then the woman and other guy all turned to each other and huddled in, talking quietly enough that I couldn't understand them. I felt so awkward so I put my hands into my jean pockets and just began looking around, trying to figure out what to do with myself.

Finally, about a minute later, they turned back to me like they suddenly remembered I was there.

The bald man spoke again. "What part are you going to audition for?"

"Not sure. What's available that I can get the music scholarship with?"

"He looks like Tristan, the lead to me," the girl said. She looked at me and seemed almost shy, but she was checking me out very carefully and scanning my body from head to toe. I guess that was part of the audition gig, but I was used to looking at people scrutinize how I ran a route, not stood in place.

"You think?" baldy asked.

She stood up and walked around the table toward me. "Yes, with that blonde hair and those blue eyes I can see him being the rocker bad boy if..." She paused and then reached her hand forward to my face and rearranged my hair a bit. "...we push his hair up like this," she finished.

The way her long eloquent fingers felt running through my hair made my body respond instantly. Thank goodness my pants weren't too tight. It had been a long time since I'd responded to a woman's touch that way. It was so unexpected and my brain was instantly off into a rockin' sexual fantasy, not an audition for a musical.

"And those cheekbones," she continued, touching my cheekbones softly.

I didn't know what she was trying to do to me, but it was doing quite a number on my imagination, making me want to experience that touch in a lot more places.

"He's definitely rock star sexy," she said. She lifted up my shirt and began to touch my stomach. Now I was feeling a bit odd. She certainly had some audacity. I should have been put off, but I wasn't. The way she did that was such a turn on. She was confident and sexy.

Her hand lingered on my chest, just above my waist line and she turned to the two men and continued talking. "This stomach…flat and hard, hard enough to…"

She didn't finish and the attractive guy in his late 20s or early 30s who'd had the dark hair and wore a suit coat came up next to her. "So, this boy is the one you want for Tristan, Fiona?" He put his arm around her shoulder and looked at her. He was observing her observing me.

"Tristan had to be drop-dead gorgeous, have a hard bod, be fit, and definitely command the stage. Unless he sings like crap, this guy can definitely do that."

The guy turned to me. "Can you sing?"

"Decent enough," I said.

Fiona kept talking. "This is the type of guy that'll make all the ladies want to throw their panties at him and become groupies. He's memorable and he…evokes emotion, let's just say." Then she looked me in the eyes and added, "Hayworth has it all."

Damn. You make me want to tear off your panties with my teeth.

The guy kissed Fiona on top of the head, almost fatherly like, but it seemed to mean a bit more than that in my opinion; like he was staking his claim. "If he's the one you want as Tristan than I'm fine with it."

"Naturally we need to hear him sing first," the bald guy piped in. He actually had a point, but I wasn't going to complain. I was relieved that I was going to be picking up a new scholarship. That was why I was there first and foremost. Remembering that when I felt like a certain something in my pants was ready to explode after my encounter with the sizzling hot Fiona was challenging, but I could take care of that later.

Rock Hard Love Hard (Rock Hard Musical #1)

"What are you going to sing?"

"How about Nickelback's I Want to be a Rock Star."

"Perfect," Fiona cooed. She went over to the piano, sat down, and began playing. "I guess we won't need this."

I belted it out and felt good enough with it. When I was done, Fiona nodded in approval and the other two guys seemed satisfied.

"Well, if this is the Tristan my talented director wants than that is who you're going to get," the guy in the suit coat said. He took her long black hair and gently twirled it between two fingers as his eyes gazed down on her clearly completely taken by her.

I couldn't help but watch the two. They clearly were a couple. However, that didn't have me surprised half as much as the fact that I was lusting after my director and I'd just met her. How was I going to manage to stay composed for months of preparation for the musical? At the moment, I just wanted to toss her onto my bed and fuck her all night long until the sun began to rise.

Fiona extended her hand out to mine. "I'm looking forward to working with you, Hayworth James." We paused, neither letting go of the other's hand first.

"As well as I," the "other guy" said. He put his hand in, causing Fiona to pull hers away. When he shook my hand he made sure he delivered one of those handshakes that were meant to send a message…he's the man and I'm…well, I'm the rock star now.

CHAPTER 2

<u>Fiona</u>

I was so distracted, thinking about my day. As my fingers ran over the piano keys casually, I couldn't get the auditions out of my mind. It had been a long journey, for certain, but what an unexpected surprise it had been that day. I couldn't have been more thrilled to finally tackle the last piece of my musical's puzzle – the lead man. Hayworth James was going to be perfect. He was memorable and sexy, too damn sexy for my own sanity, I feared. You didn't meet someone with those cocky arrogant good looks every day that could also sing, act, and make you wish he'd take you right on the spot. I could feel his intense energy, sexual and creative, so close to me. That was what I was looking for in my rock star. Someone who can rock the stage, send crowds of women and men even wild with frenzy.

Hayworth had It, and even standing next to him, feeling his body with my hands, was enough for me to want a taste of him. He was perfect.

Finally, all the time I'd invested into preparing for Rock Hard, Love Hard, was coming to fruition. It was going to be amazing and the role of Tristan was going to be one of the most memorable ones ever. I sighed, thinking about all the sacrifices I'd had to make to get to this point. All that had been missing was the fantasy man who could meet my expectations for the lead man; the one worthy enough to play Tristan. Now that the problem was solved it was time to start practicing and really bring my vision to light. It would be a few more intense months and then it would be time – it would all come together.

"Here you are, Fiona."

Michael.

Rock Hard Love Hard (Rock Hard Musical #1)

I turned my head slightly, nodding to him, but kept playing softly. Yes, he was the financier of my musical and my lover. This day never would have come without him and I knew that. He'd put up with me for the endless hours of viewing footage of actors, looking at headshots, and listening to demo tapes of those who thought they could sing. He'd massage my shoulders as I lamented about those who had the voice, but not the look, or had a good look, but no voice. It had meant everything and the fact that he was absolutely enamored by me didn't hurt either. With Michael, I had a partner that I cared about and the resources to bring my vision to reality.

Michael reached down and around, kissing my neck gently, and showed me what it was that he wished to do. I didn't mind. He was sexy, very handsome, and had a certain charm and animal magnetism, but I was starting to fear that I was becoming more than his play toy. I didn't want to be with a man who wanted to settle down and possess me. There was no time for that and although he'd been helpful, even securing me a teaching job at USC after the musical, I didn't want to be the one they pointed to and thought: she's there because of Michael Bailey, not her skills.

He took his glass and rubbed it against my neck, making my skin tingle from the chilliness of the ice cubes. I stopped playing, gasping at the shock of it and turned around. He was smiling at me coyly with his hand extended with a scotch on the rocks.

"Feeling good?" he asked.

I sipped the drink casually and set the glass down. "Yeah, glad to have found my Tristan."

"Good," Michael said. He took his glass and slid it to the inside of my blouse. I felt the moisture from the glass trickle down my chest, tickling the top of my breasts and giving me shivers from its chilliness. A soft moan escaped my lips and I could see my hard nipples poking out through my sheer bra and blouse.

Rock Hard Love Hard (Rock Hard Musical #1)

Michael's arm reached across me and he set down his drink on the piano and then guided me around with his strong arms so I was facing him. I looked into his hazel eyes and saw what he wanted. He was hungry for me, wanting to feast on me and plunge into me. Devouring me was his pleasure and it did make me feel good most of the time. It was a look that I'd usually received great pleasure from and welcomed from him. He knew the right things to do to instantly bring me pleasure.

With slow and masterful precision, he began to unbutton my blouse, letting it slide to the floor. My back was pressed against the piano and it made my breasts jut out. With one motion he released the front clasp of my bra and he slowly slid it down my shoulders until it joined my blouse on the floor.

Kneeling in front of me, Michael kissed and nibbled at my breasts, transporting me to the feelings of arousal that he's taken me to before. Then he slowly slid down and put his hands underneath my skirt, sliding it up and encouraging me to lift my hips so it would slide over them and rest on my waist. He kissed the inside of my thigh, making me moan again, this time more loudly. As his tongue darted in and out, delivering pleasant thrills through me I leaned my head back and accepted his touch, drifting off into my imagination, imagining him as my true love, my made up character of Tristan, touching me and bringing me pleasure. I shuddered, feeling the slight tremor of an orgasm from his tongue as it hungrily licked away between my legs.

Michael began to murmur, knowing the words that I loved to hear. "Seeing you take control today was so sexy…so hot, babe."

I didn't say a word, but allowed him to grab for my hand and guide me to the bedroom, where we would have the final encore. As I stared out at the lights of Beverly Hills twinkling from the penthouse apartment we shared he encouraged me to follow behind, sliding my skirt down off my hips so I had to step out of it, leaving a trail of clothes that led from the piano to the bed.

Rock Hard Love Hard (Rock Hard Musical #1)

Michael unbuckled and unzipped his pants to let it fall to the floor along with my skirt. He was already ready for me, large and bulging, just the way I loved it. It didn't take long for Michael to enter into me and start rocking back and forth gently, then a little harder, pushing me physically into the bed as my entire body wandered into ecstasy. He whispered in my ear. "How about something a bit more adventurous…a bit harder?"

"Not today," I whispered as I released into the orgasm I was having.

I looked at Michael and saw that familiar tinge of disappointment in his eyes. He wanted more than what I liked to give, yet he never abandoned hope that the day would come when my *not today* would turn into a passionate *yes*.

"I'll wait then. I see that you want to do more and when you're ready, I'll be. It'll be so worth it." He kissed my lips softly, running his fingers through my hair. I could taste myself on him.

Then he slid off of me and made his way to the shower. We were going out to dinner that night. I walked over to the closet, looking at what I had to wear and deciding what I'd like to put on. My mood was so odd. I was absolutely alive with excitement at having found Tristan, but also feeling a bit melancholy about Michael ruining my feelings of elation with yet another request for harder sex. Why he didn't accept no for a final answer was bothersome, but as long as he respected my wishes everything would remain just fine.

I decided on a black halter dress and went into the bathroom. Watching Michael shower was always kind of a thrill. He had such a hard taught body and I got to enjoy it through the glass walls of the shower too, knowing that he was also watching me get ready. It was a little game we had, a kind of foreplay, and it suited me well. I was used to men watching me and studying my body; longing for my body. However, it wasn't something that I gave away freely.

Michael was standing on the bath matt with the towel loosely wrapped around his waist, staring at me as I closed the diamond clasp that held my dress together. I spun around and looked at him.

"What do you think?"

"I think you're exquisite and divine. Perfection."

I smiled. I knew that Michael meant that and he was the type of man who demanded to be around exquisite and divine things. "Thank you."

"We're headed in a great direction, Fiona. I couldn't be more pleased."

I smiled, not responding to the statement and walked out of the bathroom and back into the living room, where I made my way back to my scotch on the rocks and took a sip of it. I was back to thoughts of the musical and the start of rehearsals, which were just a few days away. No matter what it took, I was going to ensure that this musical was a success and Rock Hard, Love Hard, would be the next great modern day musical, the one that was talked about for generations to come, reaching every stage and being made into a movies. I would stop at nothing to ensure that happened.

CHAPTER 3

<u>Hayworth</u>

It was time to make it happen and begin my musical career. All the details of the scholarship had been worked out, and I was caught up on the schoolwork I'd missed out on, finally ready to bring out my artistic side. *And to see her.*

The bald guy, whose name I still didn't know, was up at the front of the theater; shouting out something to someone whose head was peeping out from the curtain on the stage. He looked over and saw me.

"Hay, good to see you. Come over here."

I made my way down there and he looked at me. "Hay, meet your band, The Granite Gods: Ferro, Jerome, and Pittsburgh…Guys, this is Tristan."

We all assessed each other and I saw three guys that were considerably more experienced in musical theater than me. It made my confidence waver, something that I wasn't particularly used to. Ferro was the dark-haired brooding bad boy type. Jerome was the chiseled jaw dark skinned complex slick-looking one. Pittsburgh had the baby face with sandy brown hair. Together, we were The Granite Gods – the most badass fictional band ever assembled.

The guys started jamming, easily commanding their instruments. I watched them all, impressed with their skills and a bit nervous that I could pull off the same thing as the lead rocker. What was that that Fiona had said? Something about groupies and panties. She'd lost me at the panties because my mind had immediately had drifted to hers.

Rock Hard Love Hard (Rock Hard Musical #1)

I quickly found out that Baldy's name was Dan, but I still had him nicknamed Baldy in my mind and that's what stuck. He was the music director so he'd be doing a lot with us as a band, getting us organized, in sync, and sounding like a legit band.

"Let's rehearse the songs, starting at the top with Good Girl Goes Bad," Baldy called out.

We all began to do our thing to make it work and man, it was rough. We didn't mesh together well at all and it took a whole lot of patience on our part to get in sync with everything. I had no right to say my way was the best because music wasn't my main gig. However, the other three were all clearly musically inclined and they had their opinions. For me, memorizing the lyrics wasn't all that challenging and that was what I had to worry about. However, keeping up with the music beats, which I really couldn't read well, was. In a few hours' time, we managed to get the hang of it all and get through all the songs. It sounded okay; definitely more promising than when we started.

It was clear that everyone had taken their role seriously in the musical and that was a good thing. This role was important to me for reasons that extended far beyond culture and theater. It was my meal ticket so I could continue college without having to work two jobs plus take on the massive homework load at the same time.

One thing that had bummed me out was that Fiona hadn't shown up at all that day. I thought I'd see her and I was looking forward to it too. I hadn't been able to stop thinking about how much I wanted to have sex with her. I'd do whatever she wanted to, that's for sure. She would be worth it. There were no doubts about it. Maybe it was a good thing she wasn't there because she might have distracted me and then everyone would think I sucked before we even got going.

Rock Hard Love Hard (Rock Hard Musical #1)

Baldy called out orders. "Pick it up a quarter tempo, Jeremy. Hay, glance over every once in awhile to make sure you're staying in sync with your band. Got it?"

"Got it," I called out. Then I turned around and saw her. Yes! She was there and she was walking up onto the stage like it was a catwalk and she was the model selling some famous designers clothes. So confident, sexy, and beautiful. Her eyes impacted me immediately, making me long to see what existed behind them. Yes, she was someone that I'd get to know mentally before physically if I knew where it could lead. Sounds shallow, but man, I'd be lying if I said I hadn't been a player. My hip injury was the only thing that had taken me off the market for nearly two months, but I had plenty of people willing to come help me out and give me a release, including one of my nurses from the hospital.

"Let's see what we have going on here," she said. She looked at Dan and he went off into a long explanation of what they'd been working on all day. As he spoke she eyed The Granite Gods up from head to toe, starting at Ferro and working her way toward me, where her eyes lingered on every bit of my body they explored, even settling on my crotch. To my shock and horror, I felt myself getting aroused. What type of woman could do that to a guy? Give him a hard-on just by gazing at his package. Insane...absolutely insane. I shifted, hoping that my unexpected state of arousal wasn't visible to her.

"Very tantalizing group," she said. She sounded so seductive and I looked at the guys to see if they'd responded the same way I had. They were all checking her out appreciatively as though she was the girl they all wanted to take back to their bedroom, and not like a director. But as soon as she spoke in her authoritative and confident voice, they shifted their come on poses and stood straighter. "We have ourselves a real band," she added, smiling widely. The look in her eyes surprised me. She was obviously emotionally and passionately attached to this project and her excitement was genuinely adorable. It showed a more vulnerable side of her; one that wasn't just sexy siren, but was more personal. The appeal was overwhelming, to both my mind and my member.

Fiona continued talking. "Let's hear the first song."

With a cue from Baldy, we began to belt it out, me singing lead vocals and the other guys doing back-up and instruments. When we were done we looked up at Fiona to see her response. "Not bad at all for the first day, boys."

I said, "thanks", but I heard Ferro grumble. "Damn, that was pretty good."

"I hear 'ya man," Pittsburgh added, delivering Ferro some knuckles.

Fiona heard them talking and didn't miss a beat. The sexy vixen turned all business just like that.

"Yes, it was good," she said, staring directly at Ferro and Pittsburgh, making them squirm. "Good if you were a college band. You're not. You're a rock band. It needs to be better. The Granite Gods are the hottest band in the world. They aren't college. Understand?"

"But we're playing at a college theater," Pittsburgh said.

Oh no, I thought. *The dude's out for a death wish.*

Fiona's smile had remained intact, but it disappeared at his statement. She walked up to him, almost looking him straight in the eyes, and placed her hands on her hips as she began talking. "College theater! Just because this theater is in a college doesn't mean that you're some college band that plays at the trash bar downtown for a buck. This 'college venue' is a world class venue that has had some of the best musical talents play here. So, if you want to be in a college band we'll find a new Pittsburgh. If you want to be in The Granite Gods you perform at rock star level, got it?"

Rock Hard Love Hard (Rock Hard Musical #1)

Pittsburgh was staring at her, clearly mesmerized by her intensity, as well as a little scared. "Yes, sorry," he stammered. "I didn't mean to sound ungrateful."

"No need to apologize. Just be a rock star. I'm okay with you keeping it real, but you need to know what's up. A lot is riding on this."

Now all of us were in Fiona's gaze and she continued to talk, telling us exactly what she had in mind for us and expected from us. "Look, you may think you're just college students playing a role, but you're more than that. Don't lose sight of that. You were all chosen for your role because you have a quality that rock stars possess. I want authenticity and won't settle for anything less than that. People may meet The Granite Gods in a musical, but they'll want you afterward too. Don't forget that."

"Yes, ma'am," Jeremy said. His arms were folded and he was looking at Fiona the way I probably was too. I recognized the look of a guy who was thinking about what they'd like to do with a sexy sassy woman like her. He had it – no doubt about it.

"So, let's play the song again. Sound good?" Fiona asked.

None of us answered, but we rushed around, preparing to play it again and give it our all. After just a few verses I knew in an instant that Fiona was right, it already sounded better. Her certain brand of motivational speaking had worked.

She clapped afterward. "That's much closer to a rock star performance."

"Thanks," we murmured.

"You can call it a day now. Tomorrow we'll go through all the songs in the first act and get them down better, bring the others in, and we'll start rehearsing. So…make sure you work on your lines too."

"Okay," everyone said in unison again. Pittsburgh and Jeremy looked relieved to be excused for the night and Ferro strutted by Fiona like she was the one lucky to be in his presence. What a cocky douche-bag. If Fiona realized it she didn't care.

I wanted to take one last look at Fiona, but started to walk away, not even sure what I could say and certainly not wanting to get busted with the lusty thoughts that were probably shining in my eyes. It turned out that I didn't have to say a word.

"Hay, can I have a word with you?"

"Yeah, sure," I said. I was more than happy to have a word alone with her and couldn't help but wonder what she may want. Whatever it was, I was game.

CHAPTER 4

Fiona walked ahead of me and I followed her. "Let's go back to my office," she said. I smiled, suspecting what she may mean by the invitation. If it were something about the musical she'd probably just have told me on the stage or in the theater somewhere. After all, there were only a handful of people around who might hear.

"Sure," I said. Then I watched her round ass as we made our way to the back of the theater and toward her office. It looked amazing and the little bit of sway it had when she walked was so captivating.

"Here we are," she said, swinging the door open. I looked around and saw a nice office, tastefully furnished and filled with photographs of Fiona and an older man. Must have been her dad.

Rock Hard Love Hard (Rock Hard Musical #1)

She turned around and looked at me, smiling. "Shut the door."

I did just that and could feel myself getting aroused just from anticipation. Did she know that she was so sexy in everything she did? I had a feeling she did, but I didn't care. Let her show me what she's got. I'd take anything from her.

I closed the door quickly and walked toward Fiona, who was looking for something on her desk. Her back was to me and I took off my shirt and walked up behind her, pressing against her back with my chest. My nose pressed into her hair and she smelled so good. Then I slid my arms around her waist and turned her around, ready to feel the heat of her lips on mine.

Every sensation from her touch had me distracted and I whispered in her ear. "Fiona, do you want this as much as me?"

I pressed my crotch against her, showing her how much I desired her, and slid my hands on to her breasts, squeezing them gently. They felt so good and firm in my hand. I wanted to kiss them.

Then Fiona gasped. Before I could smile from her show of desire she began to talk. "Hay, I'm sorry. I didn't call you back here for this." She said it so softly and matter-of-factly. I thought I was going to die.

"I'm sorry. I'm so embarrassed. There seemed to be real chemistry between us. I must have…"

"Misread my intentions. That's okay."

"So, why did you call me back here?"

"Your vocals are great, but I wanted to see if you were interested in taking some dance lessons. You're the star after all."

"What's wrong with my dancing?"

Rock Hard Love Hard (Rock Hard Musical #1)

"Well, it's a bit too...too...sexy for the stage."

"Too sexy? That's a bad thing?" I didn't get that at all.

"Well, it's just that it looks more like you're a male stripper or something like that. I think it'll distract from everything going on. You need to take it down a notch or two."

I ran my hands through my hair and could still feel the crimson that had invaded my cheeks lingering. It didn't help that my shirt was still off either and I had a boner that was definitely noticeable underneath my tight fitting rock star jeans. Suddenly wearing them to get into character seemed like a really bad idea.

"How do you suggest I dance then?"

"Like this," Fiona said. She began swaying her hips and thrusting them forward. I duplicated her moves and she walked up to me and adjusted my back slightly, using her hands to move my hips to the rhythm she thought they should be going.

Damn, her touch is killing me.

Then Fiona moved around and stood in front of me. "Now you need to relax. You're too stiff."

"I can't. I'm still feeling this…"

Before I could finish Fiona had her hands on my shoulders and was kneading them, trying to relax me. It wasn't my shoulders that were stiff though. She went behind me and began to massage my back, making her way down my spine. "So much tension. Let me pound it out."

I didn't know if she had changed her mind or what, but I had such a hard-on that I had to turn around and find out. It was driving me crazy. I turned my body around and smash – I felt a fist drive itself into my bulge, making me hunch over in instant excruciating pain. It felt equal to what had happened with my hip on the football field. "Holy crap," I said through clenched teeth.

I could barely look up, but when I glanced at Fiona I saw that she was mortified. "I'm sorry. I was trying to pound the knot out of your lower back. You turned around."

"It's okay," I whispered.

"How did it get so hard? Did you take something to make that happen?"

Was she really that innocent and unaware of the power of her sexuality on guys like me or was she teasing me?

She reached down and started to massage it, my massive hard-on, like that would help. "I'm so sorry, Hay."

I didn't know where to look or what to do. When I felt my zipper coming undone and my raging hard-on popped out, Fiona began to rub it. "It looks swollen. It's so huge, maybe if I put ice on it, the swelling will go down. I just can't believe it," she said.

"Me either."

"What can I do?"

"You already said the most effective option isn't one at all," I grunted. "Oh my fucking... your fingers, what they're doing to me," I clenched my teeth, trying to hold it together. She was running her fingers up and down my super sensitive cock, not exactly pumping, but causing me to twitch. "That feels so good...so much better, Fiona." She was stroking me and I didn't think it would have been possible, but I was still getting harder by the second despite the pain and massive size I'd already engorged to.

"I agree, it is," Fiona said, staring down at my penis and stroking it.

"Keep it up. I can't hold on any longer, Fiona. I'm almost there."

Then she stopped just like that as if what she was doing, holding my cock in her hands and stroking me, finally hit her. "Oh sorry, I wasn't thinking."

What was this woman's deal? Torture...rough stuff. I had been wrong. I couldn't take her doing whatever it was she wanted to do. I was going to burst and I needed to release it – now!

"I've got to finish this off and leave with what little bit of dignity I have left," I mumbled, barely able to get out the sentence. It hurt to talk even.

"Can I help?"

"Privacy or your hand. Take your pick," I said.

"How about talking? Maybe it'll calm it down."

I decided I had nothing to lose at that point. I was standing there naked in my hot director's office with a raging hard-on. My body had never been such a source of discomfort or made me feel so awkward before. I was at a loss.

"So, tell me about yourself, Hay. Why did you really want the role of Tristan?"

"Man, this is awkward. Me talking about myself while trying to get off? I don't think it's going to work."

"I think it can," she said. "I don't have much time though. I have to meet Michael for dinner and I better not be late."

"That really doesn't help. What's the deal with you two anyway?"

"Now I'm the one who feels awkward," she said, laughing. "I'm watching a man try to get off as I talk about my boyfriend. I'd rather hear about you."

"Not much to tell. Got hurt during football, needed to get a new scholarship, and here I am – in all my glory I might add."

"You have an impressive glory," Fiona said.

"Not helping," I said. My hand was moving faster and faster, trying to release so I could just be done with the horror of the moment. I'd stare at her and then close my eyes, not sure how to do this. It certainly wasn't the way I'd ever gotten off in front of a woman before. They either stroked it or blew me. That was how I got off in front of women.

Then Fiona, as if she'd been watching a clock said, "Oh, I've got to go. Stay as long as you need. I'll see you tomorrow."

With that, she ran out of her office and left me there with my dick in my hand and my mind absolutely dazed and confused by what I'd just endured. I sat down on the couch and focused on a picture of Fiona. She was standing alone in front of a palm tree, wearing a sexy sundress. I imagined reaching under her dress, pulling down her panties, and pounding into her, and I used that image to bring me my release. Then I realized that I had nothing to wipe it off on and so I had to use my boxers, which I just tossed into the bathroom of the theater as I left and made my way home sporting commando and feeling confused.

The entire way home I couldn't help but wonder what had just happened to me. What had I read wrong? She seemed hot for me and then cold? What type of tease was she? I knew that I'd better watch out. I may have wanted Fiona, but I also needed this role for the scholarship too. I couldn't risk getting kicked off the cast due to some

Rock Hard Love Hard (Rock Hard Musical #1)

sexual mishap no matter how enjoyable sex with her would be.

CHAPTER 5

Fiona

I was running late and had to hustle. Keeping Michael waiting was one of the few things that he didn't have much patience for with me and I couldn't blame him. I didn't like to be kept waiting either. It was rude and annoying. Some people may have time to wait around like that, but I wasn't one of them.

The elevator to the penthouse seemed to be moving extra slow because I was in a hurry. The doors opened up and I bolted out of the elevator, briefcase in hand and bag slung over my shoulder.

"There you are," Michael said, glancing down at his watch. He looked back up at me and I saw that he wasn't too concerned. It was easy to tell by the way he looked at me.

"Sorry about that, just had to put a little motivation into the cast," I said, leaning in and giving Michael a lingering kiss on his full sexy lips. He really was a gorgeous man and the way that he looked at me often startled me with its lustiness.

"If anyone can motivate and bring out the best in anyone they set your sights on…it's you," he said, making me smile.

"You have a wonderful way of knowing the perfect things to say at just at he right time," I replied. "Just give me ten minutes and I'll be ready to go. When do you expect the driver to get here?"

"No driver. We're going to take the Jag tonight."

"Really?"

"I figured why not. It's a beautiful night outside. We might as well enjoy it. I just hope I can keep my hands on the wheel," Michael said.

"At least one anyway," I said, laughing. "Can't wait." I loved going in the Jag with the top down, feeling the rich supple leather against my legs and back. It gave me a bit of a sexual rush all in itself, plus the exhilaration of the fresh air, which ran abundantly through the meandering hills of Beverly Hills.

I went into the bedroom, quickly assessing all my dresses and hoping to find the right one for the night. I'd definitely need a wrap if we were taking the Jag. I looked over and saw the beautiful silk wrap, black with embroidered red rosebuds on it, that Michael had recently gotten me on a trip to Hong Kong. Yes, it would be perfect. I hadn't worn it yet and had been longing to. Now, what dress should I wear with it? I decided to go with my red silk dress. It was definitely a pleaser, accenting the gifts I'd been endowed with. It had a plunging neckline, sparkling ruby colored gems adorning it and creating a trail that led down the front, landing just short of my place of pleasure. The perfect accessory would be the new black strappy heels I'd gotten – they were sexy, divine, and made my already long legs really extend out. Plus, they made me a bit closer in height to Michael. I was tall, but he was a good head taller than me. I liked to look into his eyes when he spoke, finding their intensity to be most captivating and alluring. That was the one area we were most similar. When we were passionate about something it showed in our eyes, whether it was a project or idea, and the same look shone through when we looked at each other too. At times I wondered if I was more addicted to intensity or Michael. It was hard to say.

I walked out of the room and the back of my dress was still unzipped. "You mind, Michael?"

"Not at all," Michael said, walking over to me and placing his hands on my hips. His two firm and smooth hands lingered on the skin of my back, giving me shivers.

Then they slowly trailed to my backside and he grabbed the zipper, slowly pulling it up and sending pleasant thrills up and down my spine while he did so. I don't know what it was, but the excitement of this week and finding my Tristan had me feeling so horny. Admittedly, it was unusual. Where some women got off on sex for that 'sugar rush,' I got off on seeing my hard work come to fruition. The musical satisfied an inner lusty side to me that hadn't really surfaced before. It made me think that maybe, just maybe, I was ready to explore my sexual horizons on a deeper level. Who better to do that with than a very wealthy many who happened to be my boyfriend?

After the sensual way he zipped me up, Michael pressed in behind me and I could feel his taut body pressing against my back and his hot breathe tickling my neck. "There," he whispered. "Absolutely amazing."

"You always say that," I said smiling. "But thank you."

Rock Hard Love Hard (Rock Hard Musical #1)

"I would never say it if I didn't mean it. Nothing gives me more pleasure than taking you out and showing off the beautiful woman you are for everyone to see. All the men get jealous, you know. I see it in their eyes."

"That's what gives you the most pleasure?" I asked, smiling at him coyly. I didn't mind that he viewed me that way. It might tick some women off, but it was a compliment in its own way. It was nice to have someone think you were absolutely desirable.

"It gives me pleasure, yes, but not as much as the promise of what lies ahead when I get you home and peel those sexy clothes off of you one layer at a time."

"That sounds like a tempting offer…one that I can't very well refuse," I said.

"Exactly," Michael said, grabbing my silk warp and putting it around me. "This looks as exquisite on you as I imagined it would."

"Thanks."

We walked over to the elevator and made our way down to the lobby. Everyone nodded and said good evening to Michael and I, then watched us walk out the door. The beautiful black Jaguar was out in the circle, waiting for us with the top down, and looking sleek and eloquent. The doorman opened the passenger door for me and let me in as Michael went around.

"Thanks, Stan," I said.

"My pleasure, Miss Wilde."

Then we took off and Michael floored the gas pedal, sending a rumble through the car that vibrated everything ever so subtly, making me feel aroused from its power. I chuckled, thinking that it was a vibrator on wheels; an expensive vibrator at that, having a V12 engine with over 400 horsepower of rumble that was always waiting to be unleashed.

Rock Hard Love Hard (Rock Hard Musical #1)

Once at the restaurant we got to take advantage of an amazing view that overlooked Franklin Canyon and was completely beautiful and intimate. The ambiance, the staff, the fragrant smell of wild flowers and nature in the air, plus the brilliant colors of the dimming sky was all enchanting. The sun had just finished setting, leaving trails of deep red, pink, and gold glimmering in the once blue sky, making it so romantic and ideal. It was picture perfect. If I could find a way to transport that to my musical set I'd be able to set up one hot love scene between Tristan and the lead lady, Poppy. *Or me.*

With a plate of oysters on the table, a bottle of exquisite red wine that was hand selected for Michael by the chef with the promise of, "I assure you…it'll bring out the flavors of the oysters and evoke your passions." Well, one taste and we both agreed that the chef was right. Nothing short of an earthquake could have distracted us.

"So, tell me about how the rehearsals for the past few weeks have been going? I haven't been able to get down there to watch. It's unlike me, but I know that the show's in very capable hands."

"It's going well, not that I'm going to let them know it. I want them to stay hungry for improvement, work as hard as they can. This musical means too much to not expect everyone to give their best, and then some."

"Very smart move, Fiona; something I would do myself," Michael said. "Everyone doing well in their roles?"

"I think so. The Granite Gods have real potential. I can see this thing going much further than the USC theater."

Michael reached over and grabbed my hand, squeezing it gently. "That's exactly what I've been thinking too. You've invested far too much emotionally and physically to not have the production reach its full potential."

I looked at him and smiled. I really didn't consider it our musical, but I knew that without Michael it would not be what it was, which was shaping up into something pretty amazing. He continued on. "I've been talking to some associates in the business, telling them about the musical, and they agree with me that the show has potential to go international. Maybe start in New York, Rome, London, Dallas, Seattle – cultural hotspots like that. Would you like that?"

If there was ever anything that Michael could say to give me an instant orgasm that was it. "I'd love that. It's been my goal all along. I know if this show goes great the potential will be amazing."

"If anyone can pull it off, it's you," Michael said.

"Your help doesn't hurt," I said. I knew Michael knew that he was significant in making my dreams start to happen with my musical and the more I let him know that and stroked his ego, the more he'd do to help me any way he could. He always had the subtle hints to show he felt that way, including what he'd just said a minute ago. It was kind of flattering though because it meant that the musical was also important to him. Why would he invest so much effort and money into it otherwise?

"Then again, perhaps I should leave you here," he said. "The thought of being separated from you drives me crazy; thinking of another man trying to have you is torturous."

"They can't have me if I say no," I said. I shook my head briefly, shaking the undesired thoughts from my head. I didn't want them to ruin the mood of the evening. Trusting men was finally getting easier and what happened to me that day when I was sixteen never left my mind completely, but I couldn't let it dictate my future either. I deserved more than that. Aside from a great career, I knew that in the end I didn't want to go home to an empty house or shallow relationship. I wanted to go home to someone I could kick it back with, wearing no make-up, my sweats, and my hair in a ponytail. That was my type of guy! *Do you really think Michael would ever be there?* I shivered.

"What is it?"

"Just a chill," I said.

"Well, why don't we get out of here and go back home. I'm looking forward to seeing how you'd like to thank me for everything I've done to help you."

"I'm feeling creative," was all I said.

Ten minutes later we were in the Jag and making our way back to the penthouse. I couldn't wait to thank Michael by adventuring off into places he longed to go. It was new territory for me, but I could only remain more conservative sexually for so long. I trusted him too so that meant I should have nothing to fear.

CHAPTER 6

By the time we were back to Michael's, I felt ready to explode. So much intensity and desire had built up within me. The chef wasn't kidding about that red wine and oyster pairing. It had done the trick. I needed to feel him and explore new levels of my own sexuality. I was ready and I was eager. We walked into the lobby and I could only smile at everyone, feeling like what I wanted was clearly written across my face. I didn't care though.

Once the elevator doors shut I didn't hesitate to show Michael that I was willing to go farther that night than I had before. I lifted my leg up on the railing that lined the elevator, showing that I was just wearing my string thong and a garter with stockings on it underneath the red sheer fabric of the dress. I stared at Michael as I moved my hand down to play with myself. I was already so wet and revved up, ready to be pounded good and hard…not to mention have the experience of Michael doing whatever else to me. It was sure to be a new experience. I knew that much for certain. I'd even vowed to not say no if at all possible and show Michael I trusted him completely with everything in my life. It was a big step and not meant as a commitment of love, but as a bold step to show that I had trust in another person. Who better than someone who clearly lusted for me and longed to possess me in some way?

Michael stared at me as I thrust my hips forward, feeling the trembles of an oncoming mini-orgasm. My other hand grabbed one of my breasts and I slid it out of my bra, pulling it up to my mouth and kissing it aggressively. It was alert and aroused by my own tongue, making Michael groan. "Geez babe, that's hot," he mumbled.

Then I heard the elevator give the small ding that meant we'd arrived at our destination. I immediately collected and composed myself and walked into the penthouse.   Michael followed and turned around and locked the elevator before turning around to me, showing that he had needs that he was looking forward to fulfilling with the use of me.

"I'm all yours," I whispered.   Michael didn't hesitate and came up to me and turned me around, pressing me against the elevator doors and began to run his hands up and down my thighs, unlatching my garter as he did so. Then he knelt down and peeled down my stockings with his teeth, lingering on my toes as he slid each one off.   He nibbled them sensually, making my wetness skyrocket.   It was amazing and I was absorbed in the pleasure of its sensation.   Each toe tingled and nerve endings that I had no idea existed in a toe sprang to life, begging to be touched by his sensual tongue and erotic nibble again.

Then Michael made his way back up my body, kissing my inner thighs and grazing my eager loins with his lips as he continued on up until he was kissing my lips passionately and desperately.   His hands slid around to the back of my neck and he unhooked the clasp that held my dress up, leaving my sheer black silky bra showing. As he kissed my neck his fingers unhooked the clasp of my bra and I felt such relief at my breasts springing free. I longed to feel his touch.

As he kissed me, his hands then traveled down to my hips, where he unzipped that zipper he'd just helped me with a few hours ago. My dress slipped down to the ground and then he slid my panties aside and put his fingers into me, plunging in and out like it was a cock, making me groan out my satisfaction.

I slipped my hands forward and unbuttoned his gray silk shirt and slid it off, revealing one of the sexiest set of abs that I'd ever seen, and then my hands went down, sliding just under the waist of his pants, where I felt his hard-on with my fingertips. I quickly undid his belt and unbuttoned and unzipped his pants, sliding them down, along with his boxers, revealing the physical evidence of how much he wanted me.

Rock Hard Love Hard (Rock Hard Musical #1)

In one forceful and determined thrust, Michael came forward and inserted his raging hard-on into me and began to pump me forcefully, keeping my body pressed against the cool chill of the elevator doors. He kept going and going, pinning my hands up over my head as he showed his urgency. Nothing was going to stop him and I wanted to feel more. I could feel the intensity building and the little climax I'd had in the elevator was nothing compared to how my body was about to respond to his fervor.

Then, just before my climax shattered my aching loins, he pulled out of me, whispering that he wanted to take me to the bedroom and finish what he'd started. I had not realized that I had been holding my breath, but when I breathed in a small groan of frustration erupted from within me. He was teasing me and it felt ruthless. Whatever the male version of a cock tease was called, Michael was it at that moment.

He kicked off his shoes and we left his pants where they were, right next to my clothes, and made our way to the bedroom. He guided me, showing that he was in charge and I needed him. He set me down on the bed and I leaned back, placing my arms behind me and looked up into his eyes.

"Are you grateful that I'm going to arrange a tour for you?"

"Yes," I said, hearing my heart pounding in my chest.

"How grateful?"

"Very, Michael."

"Show me."

"Yes Michael," I said. I would show him how much I appreciated what he'd done for me.

Rock Hard Love Hard (Rock Hard Musical #1)

I stood up and gently guided Michael down onto the bed and he leaned back as I knelt down in front of him. My tongue slowly teased him, tracing small circles along his inner thighs as I made my way up to his beautiful cock. I'd just barely flicker his balls with my tongue and then I'd shy away, teasing him with the promises of what was to come.

His body shuddered from my actions, making me feel oddly liberated and desiring to show that I was grateful, that I had what it took to give him any kind of earth shattering hard core sex he may want from me. I trusted him and he'd taught me so much…I didn't owe anything to him, but I wanted to give him the treat of being my first with this kind of experience and let him feel how stimulating he was to me.

Finally, my lips, still adorned in bright red lipstick, slid down on his cock and I began to suck, using my tongue to stroke his girth as I moved up and down, opening my throat so he'd slide all the way into my hungry mouth and it would be enveloped in me. I moved quickly, then slowly, feeling so great from the experience. I could feel bits of his release starting to seep out of him, making my hormones go into overdrive. Everything about him was my pheromone, my turn-on.

"Fi," Michael mumbled, making me open my eyes and look up to his face, which looked wild with desire.

"I am what you please, Michael. I'll do whatever you want me to."

Michael opened his eyes and looked at me, smiling wickedly. Then he sat up more erectly and slid his hands around my waist, squeezing my ass within their firm grip. Smack. He hit my butt cheek hard, making me jump from surprise.

It stung, but it was oddly arousing. Then he began to nibble at my nipple aggressively, smacking me again, and savoring my reaction to his every move. Every part of my body felt alive, eager.

Rock Hard Love Hard (Rock Hard Musical #1)

"More?" he asked.

"Yes, more," I whispered, barely able to get the words out. Oh my god, it was so amazing, much more satisfying than I'd ever thought it would be. Intense. Animalistic. Guttural. It was everything that I had trapped inside of me that had been longing to escape. It was the physical manifestation of the passionate thoughts of my mind...the new frontiers I wanted to explore, but were too afraid to travel to.

Michael stood up and guided me onto all four's on the bed with my ass facing him. He smacked me again, then slid his hand between my legs and stuck his fingers into my wetness again. I was dripping with desire and erupting with orgasmic explosions that rocked my world. Then his one finger slid into my other hole and I found myself receiving the intense and unusual pleasure of sensations from so many different areas that I didn't know what to do. My groans gave away my confusion combined with intense satisfaction. I was disoriented and alive.

Every one of my nerves was alert and ready to feel something new. I wanted more and bit my lip to stop my auto response of 'no' from escaping my mouth.

I arched my back as I screamed out loudly from a series of orgasms that didn't leave me completely satisfied. I was longing for more and not ready to be done until my body collapsed from exhaustion.

"I knew you'd be turned on by this, Fiona. It pleases me very much. You're good…a natural. There are so many places we can take this."

I couldn't talk and nodded my head, agreeing with every word he's said. Then, without even realizing what was happening, I ended up on my back and felt the heat of Michael's breath between my legs and he took his tongue and plunged it into me just as forcefully as he'd done with his fingers earlier and he'd done with his cock so many times when he was so eager to feel my pussy tensing up around his cock.

Rock Hard Love Hard (Rock Hard Musical #1)

It was incredible and my walls were quivering, curious about what to expect next and convulsing from the over-stimulation. My hands traveled down my stomach and I felt Michael's head and wanted to force him to go harder, deeper. My back arched and he pulled back before I could come again. "Such an exquisite dish you are, Fiona. I could eat you all day. So tasty."

Then he dove back in so quickly once again, shocking me with his urgency. Nothing was going to stop me from coming again this time and I realized that he'd slid into my other hole once again, giving me that intense jolt from its shock. It rattled me to the core as I exploded on him. Then he crawled on top of me and moved in and out, sweat dripping off his brow until he released in me, collapsing on top of me right after he was done. I could hear his heavy breathing and feel the chilliness of his sweat as he pressed against my body.

Exhausted and exhilarated, I did something that I normally would never do, I fell asleep in Michael's arms, dozing off to him playfully teasing my nipples and his body pressed against mine. It felt great and there were no thoughts clouding my mind aside from that I'd enjoyed the step that we'd taken. Now that I was out of the heat of the moment I was a bit surprised about my aggressiveness and eagerness that evening, but it had been more liberating than I could have ever expected. It was as if there was something in me that refused to allow my natural inhibitions to take over. I didn't know if it was those oysters or I'd really mentally taken my sexuality to the next level. It really didn't matter in the end. I'd tried it, I liked it, and I felt safe the entire time I was doing it.

Nodding off into blissful sleep, I heard Michael talking. At first I'd thought it was a dream, but the words I heard whispered in my ear were too real. "I normally try not to let myself get too far into my pets, but I'm afraid I'm falling in love with you."

Not wanting to hear those words and savor what I'd experienced that night, I rolled to my side and then I truly did fall into a deep sleep.

CHAPTER 7

Hayworth

I was shocked to find out just how much time and energy went into rehearsing to be a lead character in a musical. If I'd thought that it was hard work on the football field, it was every bit as challenging on the stage. In many ways it pushed me even harder because I wasn't used to it. I hadn't been in the world of theater my entire life, like most of the others that were casted in production. To make matters worse, there was a hot and sexy woman looking over my every move, giving me raging hormones with just a glance or a touch on my shoulder. Even her voice, saying something as simple as "tilt your head to the left more" made my body respond. It was downright distracting and when my love interest in the musical would read her lines with me I all too easily imagined that she was

Fiona talking to me. It was a cheap trick, but it was effective. Maybe someday she'd actually say the words to me that showed me that she wanted me. I could feel it...this chemistry between us like the way I caught her looking at me sometimes let me know I wasn't too far off base. She was just resistant for whatever reason.

"Okay, take the second act from the top. I want to see you amp it up a bit, Jerome. Pittsburgh, you need to look a bit darker. Ferro, your brooding looks more like a toddler pouting – make it more meaningful...contemplative. And you, Tristan, you just think of making love to the hottest woman you've ever seen when you sing that first song. Can you do that?"

"I can," I said. *In fact, it should not be challenging at all.*

"Okay, Got it everyone?" Fiona called out.

We all nodded and went to take our places and perform for the scrutinizing eye of our director. I stared right at her, getting into my role with little effort and testing the durability of the seams on those tight rocker pants I was wearing.

Baldy gave the queue for the music to begin and the opening notes began to belt out from my band. I moved my hand on my leg, preparing to start my vocals, and gave one last lingering look at Fiona. She was looking at me too and I was positive I saw something in her eyes. She must have realized that my stare had caught her in a vulnerable thought though because she shook her head and went back to being all business. Women were typically easy for me to read, but not her. She was one of those mysterious exotic beauties, reminding me of voodoo seduction. *Hey that would be a good name for a song.*

The rhythm of the song we were singing was so fast paced, making for action that meant traveling one end of the stage to the other, dancing along the way, and looking out into the eyes of the crowd as I did it. I know when I played football at night under the lights I couldn't always see the crowd, but I could sure hear them. Here in the theater, I couldn't see anyone out there and I could not hear them either because it was rehearsal. Yet I had to look at them like I was ready to pounce on them, drawing them into the scene. That's what Fiona said anyway. No wait, how'd she put that? I was supposed to look 'right into their souls' according to her.

Moving had become easier and the small bits of pain I had in my hips occasionally was quickly eliminated with an Aleve at the end and beginning of the day. The work was demanding and I found myself enjoying it more, thinking about how much I missed football less. All in all, my unanticipated and unwelcomed injury had ended up bringing some pretty good things into my life.

Completely wrapped up in the moment, the guys and I belted out our song like it was opening night for Rock Hard, Love Hard, and I felt more like Tristan than I had thus far, tapping into how he'd feel and the rush he'd get from hearing the applause of the fans and the intensity of belting out a song that he'd written with his band...his posse.

Before I knew it, the song was done, and there was clapping coming from the darkness of the auditorium. It definitely was not my imagination either. I could see Fiona clapping because she was on the side of the stage, but others were too. Then I heard it. It was a whistle that I recognized well. It was Billy from the football team.

"Friends of yours, Tristan...I mean, Hay?" Fiona put her hands up to her eyes, trying to see who the figure was standing in the auditorium.

"Billy from the football team. I can't see him, but I'd recognize that whistle anywhere."

"Well, we're wrapped up so go have at it. Going out for a night on the town?"

"Not that I know of," I said. I could have kicked myself. I made it sound like I had no life other than this musical and homework. I don't know why I cared either way. It's not like I cared what others thought usually, but I wanted Fiona to know that I was serious…yet I didn't want her to think that I had no social life either. I'll admit it; my thoughts were driving me insane. They were the nagging thoughts of someone who would normally annoy me.

"Good. I like my star to be well rested," Fiona said, walking up to me and putting her long fingers on my shoulder. She picked off a piece of string from on my t-shirt and tossed it aside casually. She was so close to me and I could smell her intoxicating perfume. I stared at her briefly, not saying a word. I couldn't ignore the sparkle in her eyes that I saw when she was so close to me.

Then Fiona left and I walked down to the guys, who were all looking at me with shit ass grins on their face. "Now I understand why you're so into this musical," Billy said. He put his hand out and shook mine, bracing my elbow with his other hand. Then he patted my back and howled out like he was a wolf looking at a full moon.

"Shut up," I said, punching his arm.

"Don't get me wrong. If I could sing I'd be all over that. So, you banged her yet?"

I don't know why, but his words bothered me. "No, it's not like that. She's very talented…she's the director."

Billy couldn't resist. "She turned you down, huh? I guess the player can't get played in the theater group," he said with a horrible British accent.

"Rehearsals take up a lot of time," I said. I don't know why I had to justify myself or her. "I have to respect her. This is her musical."

"Say what you want, but she's still hot," he said.

"Yeah, she is," I said. There was no sense in denying it.

"Well, if you're not interested maybe you could introduce me," Billy said. I knew what he was doing. He was testing me and thought I was full of shit. Technically, he was right because I'd do anything to have a night in the sack with Fiona.

"Well, she has a boyfriend and, man, he's a millionaire. Leaves dogs like us in the dust."

Billy laughed. "So, we're going to go down to Sully's. Interested in tagging along rock star?"

"No, not tonight. I have some scenes to rehearse."

"You don't have those all memorized yet?"

"A few lines got tweaked today. Have to get it down before rehearsals tomorrow."

"I see," Billy said. He was still grinning.

"Lose the cheeky grin, Billy."

"Or what?"

"Or I'll knock it off you," I said, laughing.

"Yeah right. Now that you have to be a pretty boy for the stage you're probably too soft to take a hit any longer."

"Want to test me and find out?"

"Still got your trash talk at least. That's good."

"Well, it was great seeing you. We'll go out after the musical's done and have a good time. For now, I've got to go. Lots to do."

"See ya' later. Coming to the game next weekend?"

"I'll try. Can't guarantee."

"Well, when you're not there we've been playing better. Maybe you're a jinx," Billy chided.

"Real funny, man."

Billy and I walked out of the auditorium and parted ways outside the building. He was on his bike and I had my car over in the student parking lot.

I took off for home, knowing I had to study for some tests and practice those new lines. It was the first time where I didn't feel like I was missing out by not going out with the guys. I was always serious about what I was resolved to do, but my commitment to the musical had actually taken me a bit by surprise. I was taking it seriously and it was all because of one woman – a woman with a ferocious work ethic and drive for perfection.

CHAPTER 8

<u>Fiona</u>

If my mind could have had any more information running through it in a given day I wouldn't have thought it was possible. That is, until the rehearsals for the musical had began. I was so caught up in the opportunity, knit-picking about every detail and making sure that I gave every aspect, even down to the minutest detail, my full attention. It was all consuming and I didn't mind. After all, you had to work hard to make your dreams come true. What I hadn't banked on was seeing the Tristan of my dreams unfold before my very eyes in Hayward James. He was the real deal – the entire package. And what a package it was! I thought everyone was perfect for the roles they'd been cast in, but he gave something a little extra to his that made him spectacular. It was hard to define and even more challenging to pinpoint, but it was there. Maybe that's what they meant by the 'it factor.'

Watching him on stage was like watching somebody undergo a complete transformation. A hot, fairly talented, jock had come into the auditions that day and fit the role well enough, having the appeal that was necessary for Tristan to have: cool enough for guys to like him and sexy and sentimental enough for women to swoon over him. Now, with Hay's hard work and dedication he'd really grown into Tristan, understanding what it was that I'd seen in the character when I created it and doing his damn best to make sure he did it justice.

I'll admit that I was so grateful that he had his friend show up after he was done with that last song today. Watching him do his thing on that stage absolutely blew me away and made me long to be a dirty little girl with him. When I'd cast him for the role I wasn't counting on being the groupie that wanted to toss her panties at him, but the thought of it was all too tantalizing. I was beginning to think that Michael had unleashed a beast when he took my sexual experiences to that next level that day. Now that I had grown more comfortable with pushing my limits sexually it had made my mind go into overdrive like I was a teenage girl who was experiencing hormones for the first time. It had also allowed me to gain the confidence to push the limits with my career and think of the things I was capable of doing on my own.

You just want to distance yourself from Michael and the words he murmured to you the other night.

Michael was out of town and I decided that I needed to go get some exercise to work out my sexual frustration I was feeling at the moment. I couldn't stop thinking about what Hay had tried in my office that first day of rehearsals. There's been a part of me that wanted to repeat that day and that had been shocking enough for me to realize. There is nothing more unprofessional than a director and their star's relationship than sleeping with them on the first day. It wasn't even in my character to do such a thing, but it had nearly happened. It was ridiculous, but yet oh so tempting. Hay was yummy and whether I liked it or not, I wanted to lick him up.

Going to the club was a welcome distraction and when I got there, I chatted briefly with a few people and then changed into my clothes, eager to get a treadmill and begin running. I had to wait about five minutes, but once I got on there I began running like my life depended on it. My ear buds were on and the music was cranked.

I kept having thoughts of the musical and my hottie-tottie star with each step I took. Every female on the cast and crew seemed to be taken with Hay, enjoying his casual personality as much as his hot body and rugged rocking voice. The guys even liked him, making him a 'guy's guy' as they say. It wasn't often that someone came across a person like that and the fact that he'd busted a hip, which brought him to me, was pure good fortune. I wasn't proud of the fact that I was glad he couldn't play football anymore for the season, but it was true that I was grateful for how I benefited from that injury. I couldn't deny that I was happy as hell that he couldn't play it anymore. With any luck, the show would go on tour and he'd agree to go too, being the one and only Tristan for Rock Hard, Love Hard for the world to see. The only person that knew his role better than him was me. Thoughts of any other Tristan ever having to step in gave me instant angst. Any other Tristan would definitely pale in comparison and I didn't savor the thought of recasting him either or using the understudy.

Unfortunately, as much as my mind wanted to stick to the business and logistics of the musical, my imagination kept going back to Hay's cock. It was the biggest cock I'd ever seen, not that I'd seen many. I couldn't imagine them coming any bigger than that though. I couldn't help but smile at the thoughts of what it would feel like in me. If size really did matter, he'd be able to shatter the orgasms that Michael gave me – and those were pretty fantastic in my opinion. You didn't have to be a pro to know what a good orgasm felt like.

I looked up at the clock and was shocked to discover that I'd been running for an hour. I leaned over to my cell and saw ten missed calls, half from Michael. I got off and wiped down the equipment and someone who'd been waiting for me to wrap up swarmed the treadmill, ready to claim it before anyone else did.

I quickly went to the locker room and changed, then rushed out to my car, ready to head home. I'd call Michael on my way home. Once I was on the interstate I called him up, using the hands free in my car, and was glad to catch him live so we could touch base.

"Hey there," I said.

"Finally," he said. "I was beginning to wonder."

"Had a great run at the gym. Have to keep in shape, you know."

"I like a woman with endurance," Michael teased.

"Well then I think you'll like me," I replied. "What do you have going on this evening?"

"I have a meeting in about ten. How about you? What are your plans this evening?"

"Oh, just relaxing and going to kick back with a glass of wine and review the script a bit. Maybe do some tweaks."

"Didn't you just do some of those yesterday?"

"Yes, but you can't review it too much."

"What isn't setting with you?"

"The chemistry between Tristan and his leading love interest."

"Too unreal?"

"Just seems forced. I'm not sure if it's body chemistry or the words. Trying to figure it out," I said.

"I'm sure you will, Fi. You're really good…a natural. Well, I've got to get going. Talk later," Michael said.

"Bye," I said. He hung up before the word was even out.

Now that I was thinking further about it, I wasn't sure if I had the focus to review or tweak the manuscript. I knew I would be virtually ineffective if I didn't release the pent-up sexual energy inside of me. All I wanted to do was take a hot shower and let my hands relieve me of what a hard-on may normally, envisioning Tristan the entire time.

CHAPTER 9

Off the phone and eager to get home, I began to make my way through the one lousy section of L.A. that I had to in order to make it to Beverly Hills. It always made me feel so uneasy, realizing how horribly some people lived as much as it made me realize how fortunate I was to have nice things in life and great opportunities. Yes, I'd worked hard to create my opportunities, but passing through this neighborhood, which only went for about four blocks, reminded me of that on a nearly daily basis.

Bump. The car started to shake and I couldn't control the steering wheel. "Damn it," I mumbled. I looked around and got out of the car, checking to see what the problem was. My back driver's side tire had a flat. I looked behind it and saw some nails lying on the ground. It reminded me of a news story I'd heard a few months back about being careful about things like that and to never get out of the car. And where was I? Out of the car.

I turned around and was ready to get back in it as quickly as possible and call for some help. At first I thought of calling Hay right away and then I realized that would be silly because I had AAA. That's what I paid them for. I didn't like how dark it was on the street either. I was next to a street light, but it wasn't working. I pressed on the handle to open up the car door.

"Hey, what's going on, chica?" I jumped, not realizing that someone had walked up behind me. Make that two people had walked up behind me and they didn't look like they were Good Samaritans either.

"Just calling for someone to change my flat," I said, trying to get in as quickly as I could.

"What's the hurry?" the other one said, pressing his hand against it so I couldn't open it up.

Rock Hard Love Hard (Rock Hard Musical #1)

"We can help you out, pretty lady."

My heart was racing and horrible thoughts flooded my mind, making me cringe. "I don't need your help. You can get going to wherever you were headed. AAA will be coming."

"We just happened to be looking for a lady like you," the one guy said. I could smell his breath laced with cheap whiskey and wrinkled my nose.

Then, like a cat pouncing on a mouse, the one guy began grabbing my breasts roughly, making me scream out in shock, startled by his aggression. "Stop it!"

They didn't stop though and I could feel four hands on me, pinning me down and going to the places that I feared them going. I recalled something I'd learned in a self-defense class once and began to shout *fire* over and over, but the guy covered my mouth roughly, hissing that I'd better just shut up and cooperate. My response: I took my knee and lifted it up, delivering a swift kick to the groin, which made the guy crouch over and groan.

"You fuckin' bitch!" He shouted, winding up. I braced myself for a punch that was definitely going to hurt, but it never connected.

I opened my eyes and saw him flying backward and receiving a swift chop to the throat as he went down. The other guy began to turn around and was greeted with a swift hook to the jaw, which made the sound of cracking bones echo in the night air.

With the lights out, I couldn't tell who was there. I was grateful they helped me, but never so happy to see who it was when they came closer.

"Are you alright, Fiona?"

I stared, blinking, and found tears welling up in my eyes. I lunged into his arms. "Oh my god, Hay. What are you doing here?" I was shaking so badly and he hugged me tightly, telling me it would be okay.

"Look, we've got to get out of here," he said.

"What are you doing here?" I was so confused and couldn't focus at all.

"I was on my way home and got your text about your car breaking down. I didn't even realize that was you or your car until I got next to you. Thankfully I got here in time."

I could only nod my head in agreement. I truly was grateful. I had forgotten that I did briefly texted Hay. I could handle a great many things, but two dangerous pricks that had nothing good on their mind were more than what I could take on solo.

"Let's get out of here."

"Should we call the cops?"

"Once we're in the car."

I got into Hay's car and smiled. I remembered older cars like this when I was in high school and hadn't been in one in quite some time. It was another reminder of how fortunate I was, but nothing was as fortunate as him coming along when he did. He literally saved my life, emotionally for certain and perhaps physically too.

CHAPTER 10

I walked into Hay's apartment building and looked around. It was typical college living and I smiled, thinking of how different our lives were, yet how raw my sexual attraction was toward him. Sexual energy had nothing to do with financial status. It had to do with raw attraction and if you thought about it, that was pretty intriguing. Add in that he was now my hero and it really got complicated. I'd always tried to be cut and dry with my emotions and decisions, but with him I felt like I walking a tightrope with a hurricane blowing around me. You just didn't know what you'd be thinking or what you would get from second to second. It was exhilarating.

We walked into Hay's apartment and I looked around. He was clearly neat, tidy, and orderly naturally.

He had no idea that I'd be coming over so he wouldn't have been able to clean the place just to impress me. *Get over yourself. He may not be thinking of you as anything other than a director.* He also lived alone, which was pretty unusual for a college student.

"Have a seat, I'll be right back," Hay said. I heard his phone ring while he was in his bedroom and he was talking about something, but he came out with a t-shirt and a pair of shorts. "These will be big on you, but it should do for now."

"Thanks," I said.

"That was the police that were on the phone just now. They are going to be coming over in a little bit to get a statement from you."

"Did they get the guys?" I asked, hoping they did. I wouldn't feel secure going through that area until I found out that two less trouble makers were around.

Rock Hard Love Hard (Rock Hard Musical #1)

He shook his head yes. "No surprise that they were wanted for a few other incidents. They won't be lurking around when we go get your car later."

I nodded and went into the bathroom to change out of my ripped clothes. I had no idea what to do with them and honestly didn't even want to see them again. I just slipped them into the bag that Hay had given me and would toss them in the trash first chance I got.

On my way back into the living room I paused and looked into Hay's bedroom. I smiled, seeing that it was full of deep browns and red tones, looking like a very masculine room, one that could only be owned by a confident and highly sexual man. I wondered how many women had been in that room, feeling the pleasure of his touch between those sheets, and then getting their hearts broken shortly after.

Musky scented candles were on the dresser and nightstand, sending their scent out into the hallway even though they were not lit. I breathed in, imagining what it would feel like to have him set me down on that bed, confident in me knowing that he could deliver pretty incredible pleasure.

"Everything okay?" Hay asked, coming up behind me.

I jumped up and turned around, with my hand in a fist.

"I'm sorry. Didn't mean to startle you."

"No, I'm sorry. I guess my nerves are shot."

"That makes sense. That was scary. Whatever I can do to help, just let me know." I looked into Hay's eyes and could see that he was truly concerned, having been startled himself by what had happened.

There was a knock on the door and Hay went over, looked through his bolt hole, and saw a police officer standing there. He opened up the door and two officers came in, a male and female, and we all sat around the table while they asked both Hay and I questions about what happened, taking notes too.

That took about an hour and I couldn't stop shaking, feeling so startled by what had happened. Then they were gone and it was just Hay and I. I thought I should get going and go wait by the car for AAA to come change my tire, but I was hesitant. What if those guys had some goons waiting for me to go back? They were probably pretty pissed off as it was.

"Do you want a glass of wine, Fiona? I've got red and white."

"Actually, that would be great. Red please," I said, smiling at him appreciatively. That sounded much better than going at the moment.

"It's probably not as good as what you're used to, but it's not bad."

"You like red wine?" I asked.

"No, but…" Hay stopped talking and it made me laugh. Apparently the lady friends he had come over to visit did like it.

We sat down, ordered a pizza, and began talking. At first it was about the musical, but then Hay began to talk about his family and the restaurant that his father had owned, but was forced to close down due to the economy.

I was so shocked to hear the name of the restaurant that his parents had owned because it was a place that I'd actually been to and I remembered it well. I'd eaten there with my dad as a little girl on a vacation. We'd been passing through that town and I absolutely fell in love with the homemade cream puffs they had, eating two that day. In fact, I'd even begged my dad until he couldn't say no to drive out of his way back home so I could get some more. I'd loved those cream puffs so much, looking so funny after

Rock Hard Love Hard (Rock Hard Musical #1)

I ate them. My face would be sprinkled with that powder sugar and white cream, really standing out.

Hay was laughing at my story, sharing how he'd never liked those cream puffs after he had to start learning how to make them when he was ten. Our conversation was great, like two long lost friends, reminiscing about life's funniest childhood memories. The only thing that stood out was the obvious sexual energy between the two of us. I could sense it in the air and almost feel it on my skin. I was looking at him and despite the harrowing experience earlier my nerves were alive with so much desire. I could not ignore it. The look Hay was giving me didn't help either because I knew he was thinking the same thing and could clearly tell what was on my mind. There was no way I was going to act out on my desires or mention them either. Hopefully Hay would take that same approach. It just wasn't a good idea although it showed promise to be a great experience if it happened.

We had sudden silence, which felt so awkward after the laughter and conversation, and I couldn't take my eyes off him. He was my sexy, all-American, Tristan, rock star, sexy man strutting the stage, guy. His lips looked so soft and I could only imagine what they'd feel like pressed against mine in a tender kiss. You know the kind…they start tender and quickly turn urgent.

It was as if everything was in slow motion. Hay leaned in closer to me and brushed my cheek softly with his finger. I knew he wanted to kiss me and I had to do something. I had to remain focused on what was most important at that moment – the musical. *How about your boyfriend?*

"I suppose I should get going. It's getting late," I said.

I saw the disappointment in his eyes, but put my head down so I couldn't see it for long or worse yet, change my mind. Leaving was the best thing to do.

Rock Hard Love Hard (Rock Hard Musical #1)

"Okay," he said. His voice was soft and understanding, showing no desire to talk me into doing something that I was hesitant to do, and I was grateful. That made him more than completely sexy; it also made him a gentleman. It was a potent mix that made me want him more. I wasn't sure if he'd just mastered the game or was naturally that good, but it was crazy. He seemed so much more mature than his age and worldlier than his life experiences should have made him.

"I should call the car service in case it'll be a bit of a wait," I said.

"I can change your tire if you have the supplies," Hay said.

"You'd do that for me?"

"Yes, the sooner we're in and out of there the better. I have no choice but going through that neighborhood, but if you have a choice you should take the long way round."

I wanted to be offended by the safety lecture, but it was surprisingly touching and sweet to me. I walked out of Hay's apartment, laughing at my clothes, and fully realizing that it looked like I was doing the infamous 'walk of shame' that many college students do, but I didn't care. I felt good that Hay was there and if a girl was going to have a walk of shame she might as well have it with a sexy guy walking next to her.

The ride over to my car was quiet, but the silence was comfortable, not awkward. We got back to my car and I watched Hay quickly change the tire, flexing his muscles, and looking completely at ease and competent with the task. I was paranoid though and kept looking around, making sure nobody was going to approach us. I walked to the other side of the car and frowned. Someone had keyed my car and that was annoying, but it was time to choose my battles and that wasn't one of them.

"All done," Hay said, slamming the trunk of my car.

Rock Hard Love Hard (Rock Hard Musical #1)

"Thank you so much." I reached in and hugged him closely. I could feel both our hearts pounding as our chests pressed together.

I got into the car and Hay stood on the sidewalk, watching me drive off and when I rounded the corner he was still standing there.

I sighed, thinking about what I'd initially planned on doing when I got home that evening. It still sounded like a good plan, but the motivation was a bit more personal than just raw sexual attraction.

CHAPTER 11

<u>Hayworth</u>

The next days were fast and furious for me. I had semi-finals to tend to with school and they took a lot of brainpower, plus the rehearsal schedule had picked up as we were getting closer to opening night. Fiona had gone all out with small adjustments and tweaks, bossing us around and able to cross that stage in her sexy stiletto's at about a hundred mile per hour speed. She was never in flats or sneakers, but I had to admit that her legs looked so sexy in those pumps that I didn't mind at all.

Glad to have an early call for rehearsal, I made my way home and was going to take a shower and learn my new lines. And to be honest, I was going to jack off too. I hadn't been with another woman since meeting Fiona and my needs were clearly not being met. While my hand wasn't what I preferred, it would allow me to alleviate my built up tension enough to focus on the tweaks in my lines that happened that day. I had to relearn some things and didn't want to fall short. Even though Fiona and I had developed a stronger platonic bond since her incident, she had no problems chewing me a new one if I dropped the ball on something during rehearsal. If she was going to chew me a new one I didn't want it to be metaphorically – I wanted to feel her doing it to me.

No sooner than I'd gotten home and went to get ready for my shower, I heard a knock on my living room door. I rolled my eyes, not feeling like talking to anyone. It was probably Billy and I didn't have time to shoot the shit with him.

I swung open the door and was shocked to see Poppy Wilson standing there. She played Shasta, my love interest in the musical and she had some of the brightest and thickest wavy red hair I'd ever seen. She was also pretty hot, someone that would be right up my alley usually.

"Poppy." I had no idea how she knew where I lived.

"Hi Hay, mind if I come in?" She walked past me, not bothering to wait for an answer.

"Sure…um…what can I do for you?" I shut the door and turned around to look at her.

"Well, I need some help rehearsing my scenes; especially the love scenes…the kissing parts."

"Yeah?" So many thoughts were going through my mind. I didn't want to lead her on and give her the wrong impression, but I just had gotten done evaluating how I was in need of some sexual gratification. If given the choice, Poppy definitely beat out my right hand. Plus, Fiona had Michael and they were a couple. I may have the hots for her, but I wasn't about to stand around waiting for her to finally break down and give me her smoking bod.

"Well, it's important for us to have chemistry, Hay." She put her finger tips on my chest and slowly moved them downward. Her long nails tickled my chest and it sent a shiver down my spine that ended by my groin, which was very alert to what may be coming its way.

"I agree…you think that rehearsing will…"

Poppy cut me off and pressed her lips against mine so I couldn't talk. Her hands wrapped around me and she pressed her pelvis forward, making my cock greet it at attention as a thank you.

Without skipping a beat, Poppy dropped to her knees, not caring that I was standing by the door to my apartment and unzipped my pants, sliding them down and having me step out of them.

"I knew it would be that big. You can tell. It's yummy."

I don't know why I felt I should at that moment, but I wanted to clarify that there was no chance for a relationship. That wasn't going to happen. "I just want to make sure you understand…"

Once again, Poppy cut me off. "I am only interested in the musical and making sure that it is nothing short of phenomenal. Without us having chemistry the show won't work. I've come too far to have my big opportunity fall short."

"So, you don't want anything else?"

"No, absolutely not," she said casually. "Don't be so full of yourself. Let me be full of you instead." With that, she put her mouth over my cock and began to give me a blow job that was worthy of a porn star, passionate and paralyzing my every attempt to be cautious and practical. I was so engorged and her mouth could take all of me, sliding me down to the depths of her throat. The feel of her throat muscles contracting around it made me tighten up and she reached around, digging her nails in my ass and holding me tightly. She was in complete control of her performance.

"I think I've got to sit down," I said. It was an odd thing to say, but I'd never had a blow job from someone who was so giving and well…experienced. It was fucking amazing. Plus, most women wouldn't take in my entire package. She could and it was a turn-on for obvious reasons.

We made our way over to the couch and she whipped off her clothes, staring at me in all her naked glory. Her skin was so creamy, and her body very curvy, sexy, but different than Fiona's. Her large breasts bounced freely. They were all natural and her rosy nipples were erect and huge, making me want to feel my lips around them.

Then she was back down, into pleasing me completely and totally. She was as ambitious as anyone might be when they were trying to please someone for a specific reason. Being the recipient of such services was a good deal. Now all I had to worry about was not exploding too soon. That would suck.

Poppy purred, whispering seductive little compliments to me. They weren't anything I hadn't heard before, but they sounded so natural coming out of her mouth. She really was a little vixen and it was pretty hot.

After bringing me close to a come, Poppy slithered up and slid on top of me, straddling her legs around me on my couch and slid onto me easily, showing that she'd been completely wet and aroused from delivering me pleasure. Once on me, she turned from sultry vixen into the rodeo girl, riding me and bucking back and forth, thrusting her hips forward, and swiveling them around on top of me. I could feel her having orgasms. Her wetness dripped on my legs, driving me crazy. Her big breasts were pressed against my face and I began to lick and bite her nipples.

Rock Hard Love Hard (Rock Hard Musical #1)

She was so carefree and it was hard not to get wrapped up in the moment.

I wanted more before I came. I picked her up, which was easy enough to do and moved her to the side.

"Lean over," I said.

She didn't argue or ask what I was going to do. Poppy was game for anything and it was a big turn-on. She didn't pretend to be a good girl. She celebrated being a girl who loved sex and that made her a prime booty call. Wait…it's actually me that's the booty call. *You idiot…why are you thinking of that right now.*

Poppy grasped the couch and I leaned in from behind and entered into her, moving back and forth rapidly, feeling her ass press against me with each movement. My hands reached around and squeezed her tits, kneading them in my hands, and making her moan.

"Yes, Tristan. That's so good. Yes, yes….yes!" She was yelling loudly and my neighbors probably wondered what was going on. It's not that they'd never heard a woman's pleasure coming from my place. She was just that wild. Her calling me Tristan was highly irrelevant…after all, this was rehearsal.

"I'm getting set to…" I groaned.

"No, not yet," she said. This chick was trying to kill me.

She got up and ran over to my kitchen counter and hopped on top, straddling her legs on the kitchen table. "Come and get me!"

I didn't hesitate. I went over there and ducked under her legs, popping up in between them. I pressed my hands on the counter and leaned in, kissing her pussy roughly and aggressively, nibbling it as my tongue slithered in and out. "That's good," she said. "Keep it up."

Rock Hard Love Hard (Rock Hard Musical #1)

Now she's playing director, I thought.

As I kept going on her quickly, feeling her juices on my face, she slid her hand down and rubbed her clit, masturbating while I pleased her. Her hips began wriggling more and she tried to send my tongue deeper into her. Poppy was insatiable.

I took one of my hands and pressed it against her ass, feeling her wetness drip onto my palm. Then I sent two of my fingers in – one taking advantage of each orifice. If this woman loved wild, she'd love this. I moved them back and forth as my tongue continued to move in and out of her and she kept on stimulating her clit. Then it happened. Her body froze and she purred. "I knew you'd be a kinky bastard. I love it."

I smiled at her, appreciating her boldness and knowing that it took a certain kind of sexual confidence to handle that move.

"Now, follow me!" She called out. Once again, she was off. She was more energetic than a rabbit, moving about quickly and with great agility. She ran down the hall and made her way into my bedroom. I followed, laughing at her eagerness and definitely feeling the need to release now. My cock had been on a long roller coaster ride and was set to get off.

"Now that I know what you like I'm ready for a little fun myself."

"What do you..."

Once again she silenced me by giving me a shockingly aggressive shove so I fell back on my bed. I was about to say something and she said, "Uh..uh...uh."

Poppy dove down to my cock again and began to suck on it, getting it as stiff as it had been when we'd first started our sexual escapades. I don't know what she was doing because I couldn't even keep my eyes open, but she had all her hands and her mouth working in harmony, like a conductor performing a masterpiece on my cock. I was shocked when I felt something slide into me – something I'd never experienced before despite doing it several times. Her other hand was caressing the spot below my balls, stroking it firmly between their and my ass and I was arching my back, feeling absolutely confused by the excellent feelings surging through me. Holy shit! This chick was a beast.

Then I noticed it was about to happen and I tried to push her away so I could slide into her. She ignored me and kept going. I didn't mind coming in her mouth. It would be worth it and I needed to do it. Just as I grunted, "I'm…" she pulled out and I ended up shooting my release all over my chest.

Her response? She slowly trickled her tongue up my torso, licking up my release like she was tasting frosting on a cake. Then she went up to my mouth and kissed me deeply, allowing it to drip in.

Okay…I didn't dig that at all, but I could hardly say a thing. I didn't exactly complain when a woman gladly swallowed my release.

"Ugh," I said.

"It's all part of the joy of it all…the raw sexual connection," Poppy said.

I don't know that I agreed with her, but I didn't say another word.

"Well, this has been fun. A great start to rehearsals. I best get going. Got finals to study for. How about you?"

I shook my head yes, not even able to talk.

I followed Poppy out into the living room, still naked, and watched her get dressed. She talked away casually, mentioning the musical and complaining about people that I had no idea who they were.

Rock Hard Love Hard (Rock Hard Musical #1)

"Well Hay," she began. "That was a good start. I don't think there'll be a problem with our sexual energy on stage. You may want to work on that endurance a little though."

What? Ouch? Was she kidding? I couldn't have held it a second longer after that masterful manipulation of my man muscle.

"I'll keep that in mind," I said. I think I was actually a bit crimson from the comment. Maybe it was just being flushed from having one of the wildest and most unexpected sexual encounters of my life. Then a thought occurred to me: maybe that was the way it really was for rock stars.

"Well, see you tomorrow. Ciao, Hay."

"Bye Poppy."

With that she was gone and I could hear her phone ringing. She answered it. "Oh hey, Mom....yeah, I was just rehearsing."

If her mother only knew. Feeling some serious gratification, I went into the bathroom to take my shower and then really did get down to studying and looking over my lines. Concentration came easily and I had my co-star in the musical to thank for it. The next time I looked up at the clock two hours had passed and it was time to go to sleep.

CHAPTER 12

Fiona

I was eager to wrap up practice and take off to Napa for the weekend with Michael. We'd both been working so hard on our various projects, him organizing a tour for the musical and me making sure that my cast, crew, and set were ready for opening day. We hadn't seen very much of each other and I missed him.

"We can call it a day," I shouted out to everyone. Although they wouldn't admit it, I could tell that my entire crew was equally grateful for a weekend reprieve. It had been productive and necessary, but chaotic too. Basically, I'd had no life outside of the production and as a result, my cast and crew hadn't either. At least I didn't expect from them what I was not willing to give myself.

Everyone started to clap and I smiled at them. "Have fun, but not too much fun!"

I couldn't help but notice that Poppy had strolled over to Hay and grabbed his ass, thinking she was all sneaky. Actually, she wasn't trying to be sneaky at all. She was certainly into their onstage chemistry and I had to admit, watching them was so convincing that I was almost jealous. It got me a bit revved up too, which was why it was a great thing that Michael and I were headed to Napa for the weekend.

I felt a set of soft lips kissing my shoulder and I smiled. I turned around and looked at Michael, who was perfectly groomed and looking very handsome. It was a rare moment where he had jeans and a t-shirt on, showing off his great body because of the clinging fabric. "Ready to go, I see?"

"Indeed. I can't wait to indulge in you this weekend."

Rock Hard Love Hard (Rock Hard Musical #1)

"I thought we were going to be sightseeing?" I laughed softly.

"I know what I'm most eager to see…that face of yours as it radiates when you surrender yourself to me. More beautiful than even a Napa Valley sunset."

I saw Michael's brow furrow and I turned around to see what had distracted him. Hay was standing right there.

"Have a nice weekend, Fiona. I wanted to thank you for that advice with the fourth scene of act two. I think it'll help a lot."

"My pleasure," I said. I don't know why I did it, but I couldn't resist looking into those piercing blue eyes and getting lost in them every time Hay spoke. He was one of those guys that could recite the weather and make it sound interesting.

Michael stepped in front of me. "I haven't had the chance to thank you for coming along when you did to help Fiona the other week, Hay. I'm truly grateful."

"It's no problem, Mr. Bailey. I'm only glad that I came along when I did."

Michael extended his arm out and shook Hay's hand and I had to hold back a smile. He was shaking his hand firmly with a grasp tight enough to make his knuckles turn lightly white. He was defending his machismo and what was most important to him – me. It should have bugged me that he thought of me as a possession, but that was just his style. He treated me great and practically offered me the world. Guys didn't get to that point of success by not standing their ground. It was kind of endearing to see that he was that way with a college guy, the lead in my musical. *Apparently you're not as subtle as you think.*

Rock Hard Love Hard (Rock Hard Musical #1)

"Well Fiona, we should get going. It's a long drive and I'm eager to get to Napa," Michael said, not bothering to hide the suggestive tone in his voice.

"Of course," I said.

"Have fun and rest up," Hay called out. I looked around at him and saw the largest playful grin on his face. He was coming right back at Michael in his own style, showing his confidence by being completely casual. I laughed, but quickly hid it when Michael turned back around and gave him a curt smile.

All our bags had been packed at the beginning of the day and loaded into the car so we wouldn't have to fight as much crazy Friday afternoon traffic as we made our way for our romantic weekend. Michael had planned it all and I couldn't wait to see what he'd done. Not only did he have exquisite taste, but a real passion and flare for detail. It was nothing short of inspirational and it showed in everything he owned. I suppose I was a part of that too. Expect the best. Surround yourself with the best too.

"So, the week wrapped up good?" Michael asked once we were on the interstate.

"It was fantastic. Everyone's chemistry is getting stronger all the time; especially Tristan's and Sasha's."

"That's great, right? A charismatic lead couple is always a draw."

"Yes, I suppose," I said.

Michael glanced over to me. "Whenever you say that I know there's something weighing on your mind. What is it?"

"I can tell that they're into each other, probably been doing some rehearsing off stage."

"And, Fiona?"

I sighed. "And...I know those things can leave as quickly as they happen to arrive. I can't have them fizzle or have a fight before the show starts. That would be a slippery slope and so detrimental to my hard work...our hard work."

"It'll all work out, Fiona. Just wait and see. From what it looks like, That Poppy Wilson is a determined one, willing to do what it takes to not only get the role when she did, but to make sure that she's successful at it."

"I suppose that's why you recommended her, huh? You could see that."

"Well, I saw her talent, but the rest wasn't too hard to figure out. She's somewhat of an open book with her ambitions. And being in my position, you meet a lot of piranhas and she is definitely a piranha."

"Surely Hay could keep his cool regardless. I see the way the female cast and crew ogle over him," Michael said.

Yes, there it was. The subtle hint of the man asserting his dominance, marking his territory. "That's because he's a natural; just that type of guy. He has the most to lose by the show not going well so I don't worry about him."

"Like what?"

"His scholarship. He couldn't afford to be at USC without it. After the football injury, it was actually his coach that led him to us, remember. Thank you to that coach."

"Well, this is supposed to be a weekend about us escaping, having some fun, and forgetting about work for awhile. Recharge our batteries," Michael said. He reached his hand over and squeezed my leg gently.

Rock Hard Love Hard (Rock Hard Musical #1)

"You're right," I said. We were quiet for a minute as I tried to rewire my mind to talk about something other than the musical. I was kind of like a broken record as of late, thinking and talking the same thing. I may say it in a different way, but it always came back to the musical and how much I wanted it to be a success.

Finally, I'd blocked out thoughts of the musical. Michael and I talked casually as we meandered northward toward Napa, enjoying the views of the Pacific Ocean as they peaked out of nowhere from time to time. It was such a beautiful ride, one that I'd only taken a time or two before with friends.

The sky was bright blue as we went and had some white clouds rolling along in it. They were so billowy and calming, reminding me of a really soft down comforter. Then the winds that blew off the ocean would pick up and send the clouds drifting away until they evaporated above the ocean or were out of sight.

We made a pit stop and got a cup of coffee to enjoy on the way and help keep the chill of the ocean air off us. Between the heated seats of the car and the java it worked wonderfully. Every once in awhile I'd reach over and casually play with the top of Michael's hand as it rested on the knob for the stick shift. He'd look and smile. It was actually really nice and I was surprised at how much I was at peace with the thoughts of us being a couple that was maybe falling in love. Maybe it had been good to get away and separate myself from the musical. My passion for it was certainly different than my passion for Michael. I could see that more clearly now that I'd gotten some distance from it.

I noticed Michael glancing over at me with a wry smile on his face and I looked down to see what he was looking at. I'd only been hoping I hadn't dripped a bit of coffee on my t-shirt, but I quickly found what had him so amused. My nipples were so hard, responding to the ocean breeze and the invigorating ride. I couldn't hide it.

Feeling playful, I said. "That's not the only thing aroused." I winked at Michael and he smiled. Then he pressed down the accelerator and passed a series of cars at lightning quick speed. I pressed my free hand down on the seat and felt the g-force of the car pressing my body back into the soft lustrous leather. When I glanced over at the speedometer, I saw that we were going about 100 miles per hour. That car was rugged power and masculinity, almost exactly like its owner.

The ride had gone surprisingly quick, taking only five hours instead of over six due to Michael's aggressive driving. "We're here. Record time."

"Eager?" I asked.

"You'd better believe it, Fiona. This promises to be a *very* special weekend."

Michael came around and opened my door up and we made our way into the bed and breakfast that we were going to be staying at. It was so enchanted looking; a huge home that looked like it had been taken right from the mountains of Italy. Green vines grew upon its stucco sides, stopping just short of the cedar accents. The entire front that led into the entrance was cobblestoned and quaint. Statues were off to the sides, some fully exposed and other subtly hidden among various flower beds or other landscaping features.

Once we walked inside I saw a tastefully and simply decorated romantic paradise. This was the type of place you'd find in a movie scene...the scene were the climax of the story took place and the two lover's who'd constantly missed each other finally collided like two stars in the night, creating an intense explosion that could be seen and felt around the world.

"Hello Mr. Bailey, we're glad that you will be joining us this weekend," a lady said. She was poised, slightly plump, and had a genuine, merry smile upon her face.

"Miss Wilde and I are looking forward to it very much," Michael said. He turned to smile at me and I smiled back, feeling an unexpected surge of shyness.

"Wonderful. Here's your key," she said.

I couldn't hear what he was saying, but Michael leaned in and whispered something to the lady. She giggled and smiled, nodding her head yes. Then I saw him slip her a hundred dollar bill and we were off to our room, following the man who'd just walked in from outside and was holding our bags.

We followed the man up the stairs to a room that faced the backyard of the bed and breakfast. He opened the door and stood aside, letting Michael and I walk in first.

"Where would you like these, Mr. Bailey?" he asked.

"You can set them over there," he said, pointing to a row of dressers in the far corner.

The man hustled over and found himself greeted with a hundred dollar bill by Michael too. I was impressed. He was always generous with people he liked, but the grand tips seemed a bit excessive. For some reason he was really sparing no expense and making sure I noticed it.

Michael walked the bed and breakfast staff guy back toward the door and stood to the side so he could leave. He closed the door right afterward and turned the lock before staring back at me with some expressive eyes. "So, welcome to the weekend," he said to me as he turned back around.

I smiled and didn't skip a beat. I was eager to make love with him…nothing rough, but just feel his hands on my body and mine on his, enjoying the way we connected.

With my t-shirt off, I began to playfully unzip my jeans, leaving my strappy stiletto's on underneath them until I was standing in front of Michael in my emerald green bra and panties, moving my hips seductively in his direction, looking like I was ready to tango. Only this dance of love was going to be done on the sheets, not the dance floor.

"So damn sexy," Michael murmured and he came up to me and wrapped me in tightly. Feeling my body press against his was so tantalizing, so inviting, and I was instantly excited by it.

Michael laid me down on the bed and slowly took off one stiletto at a time and then slid off my panties and bra. I was lying there naked and he was staring at my body like it was a piece of art. He knelt down at the edge of the bed and began to kiss my toes slowly and methodically, sending shock waves through my body. He traveled up my long legs casually, just hinting at and teasing the part of me that was longing for him most, and continued on my stomach, licking it softly with his tongue.

I felt so incredible and desired him so much. This was perfect...so nice and slow. It was as if he'd known what I wanted and was ready to hand it over to me in the most erotic way possible.

As his hot lips seared my breasts with their touch as he kissed them, I softly moaned his name and begged him to enter inside of me.

"You want me?" he asked.

"Yes, so badly, Michael."

"All great things come in time," he said. Then he rolled me over and began to kiss me from my head to my toes on my backside, nibbling my ass gently along the way. It felt so good and better than any massage I'd ever had in my life. I could feel my muscles melting and releasing. Then they'd tense up for a bit, but succumb to his sensual moves. I soon found out that my body had no control over its responses. Michael knew every move he made was taking me further into an aroused state, a state that would lead to my complete sexual gratification.

In a shocking, but definitely turn-me-on move, his tongue flickered by my anus, sending a zap through my entire body like I'd just been electrocuted. It caught my attention and I could feel my wetness escalate in response.

"Please, enough teasing. Enter me," I begged.

"You sound sexy when you beg," he said.

I smiled and turned around underneath him. "Please Mr. Bailey, enter me and show me how powerful you are...please," I begged.

"Very well, you've been patient." With that, he entered me and began to rock back and forth like we were on a small sailboat on the ocean, not the big soft bed of the hotel room. The way he moved was pure perfection and my body embraced and absorbed every move, responding to it with my own rhythmic moving and joyful expression.

"I'm going to…" I whispered. I couldn't finish the sentence, but my orgasm spoke the words for me. Michael arched his back and came at the same time too.

"That was incredible," he said. "I needed that so badly."

"Me too," I said.

Then, as if it was an afterthought, I said, "I'm hungry…for food."

"Well, you're going to need your energy so I suggest we go take a hot tub and eat."

"What?" I asked, confused.

"Follow me." Michael grabbed my hand and led me into another room. I saw a hot tub in there that was filled and steaming warm. Next to it was a small fridge with a glass cover that had a plate full of fruit, cheese, vegetables, and chocolate, plus a few bottles of wine.

"You really did think of everything. I'm glad you did," I said.

I slipped into the tub and Michael slid in next to me. We began to eat our feast in the hot tub.

"You know, I really enjoyed what we did the other week. I've been looking forward to going a bit further," Michael said. He set down his wine glass and played with my shoulder casually.

I knew he was talking about the rougher sex and wasn't sure what to do about it. I had enjoyed what we'd done the other week. I couldn't deny it, but I wasn't so sure that I was a rough sex girl. At minimal, I didn't know if I wanted to go any further than that. It was great, but there had to be a limit, right?

"We'll see," I said with a smile. I didn't want to say yes or no just yet.

"As our relationship continues to grow, I think you'll open up to just how exciting it is to explore your limits sexually with someone you l…long to be with." I noticed the hesitation at the *l* and it was clear that Michael almost said love. Thankfully he didn't because I wasn't ready to hear those words when I was fully awake, staring at him in a hot tub. He clearly was not set to say that word either because he stopped himself.

Michael continued talking. "In a few weeks, my parents are going to be coming to Los Angeles. I'm eager for you to meet them and attend their charity event with me. Would you do that?"

"Of course," I said. "What charity?"

"Oh, I can't recall. It's something to do with children and the arts."

Rock Hard Love Hard (Rock Hard Musical #1)

"Sounds wonderful."

"And...I was hoping that you'd play the piano at the event. I know they'd love that and they'd get to see the same amazingly talented woman that I see every day."

"Absolutely," I said. I was always glad to help a charity out, but I was also aware that meeting parents was a big deal...even Michael Bailey, the playboy's parents.

Michael leaned over and kissed me sweetly and put his hand between my legs and began to rub me intimately. "You're the most wonderful girlfriend ever."

I melted at his words. He'd never called me girlfriend before and it was the first time that I felt like our relationship was more than just pleasant and mutually beneficial. Yes, I'd seen the signs coming, but in my heart of heart's I'd always just thought that it would never really happen. Now it was and I wasn't sure what to do about it.

The words he spoke made me feel wonderful, yet scared. *One day at a time,* I reminded me. Then I scolded myself for putting such thoughts in my head on a weekend that was supposed to be about escaping reality and getting away with someone I cared for, someone who was fun and adventurous down to their very core.

"Hey," I began. Michael looked at me oddly. "Shouldn't we get out of here before my skin is too pruned for you to even want to look at it, much less touch." I realized as I said the words that Michael had temporarily taken my *hey* for *Hay.*

"Sounds like an offer I shouldn't refuse, Fiona. However, if someone would look good like a wrinkly prune, it would be you."

"I drive a hard bargain." Then I looked down at his cock and saw it inflating, ready for more. "A very hard bargain."

Rock Hard Love Hard (Rock Hard Musical #1)

We got out of the hot tub and dried each other off. The way Michael blotted the wet ends of my hair was so loving and caring. I felt like a pampered princess, almost defenseless. It should have made me feel too vulnerable, but instead it had made me feel really nice – very special.

Not wearing anything, we made our way back to the bedroom. The rest of the evening was spent trying to find the limits of what I would do and would not do. At times, it was more like a seminar where I asked questions and got information to make decisions. It might have appeared comical to some, but it was a truly revolutionary moment for me in regards to trusting a man who I knew I could grow to love and releasing the inner demons that held me back from truly giving my body completely to another man.

The weekend went by entirely too fast. On Sunday when it was time to go we'd spent well over three-fourth of our time in Napa in our room and the rest was purchasing wines for Michael's private collection. It had indeed been a weekend made in heaven and one that I'd needed more than I realized. It helped to clear my thoughts and slow down the static in my mind.

CHAPTER 13

On my first day back at rehearsals, I went from relaxed casual to rapid speed. I realized that it was only two weeks until opening night and the combination of my nerves and drive for perfection made me focus on every detail, no matter how minute it seemed. It was time to set aside the high heels and dressier clothes. I wore tennis shoes, jeans, and t-shirts, slinging my hair into a high ponytail that cascaded down my back. I was all business.

The cast and crew didn't seem to mind my intense attitude, and I was pleased to see that it seemed very important to them too; that they knew my ideas and attention to detail were meant to help all of them have a successful run with the musical. Furthermore, the cast seemed to get along very well off the stage and that made all our chemistry together on stage all that much stronger.

Things were working out fantastically and the one thing I'd been concerned about – Hay and Sasha's offstage interactions (or so I presumed) – were working out. They were true professionals at rehearsals and that made me thankful that there likely wouldn't be melt-downs before or during the show's run.

That day it was time for another one-on-one with Hay to further dive into the little nuances that kept making Tristan a better character every day of rehearsals. While I was waiting for him in my office I couldn't calm my thoughts down. I'd been working so hard, only getting about five hours a sleep per night maximum, but I'd never felt so alive and energized. If I didn't love what I was doing so much I probably would have looked like an exhausted old hag, but woke up every morning feeling ready to tackle a marathon day of rehearsals. All the years of planning between writing the musical, finessing its content, planning out characters, sets, music, and every other detail in between, were finally coming close to fruition. I've never felt more excited about anything.

Rock Hard Love Hard (Rock Hard Musical #1)

As I took advantage of a quiet minute alone I stared at the clock. Tonight I have to leave early to go to the benefit with Michael and meet his parents, plus play some songs on the piano. Now it didn't seem like such a good idea and the thought of having to bust away from the musical early in order to go get all dressed up was undesirable. But it was a commitment that I had to keep because it was the right thing to do. The only real concern I had was that I could not deny the intense animal attraction I had when Hay was around.

Maybe it's because he's your hero. That's why you can't forget him. The night of the attack had been scarier than I cared to admit. Everything had turned out fine, but if Hay hadn't shown up it might have been very different. Could I have really handled the situation myself? I'd like to think I could have, but I really didn't know. How would someone know that until they experienced it?

And afterwards when I got the chance to learn more about his family and his childhood, Hay became more and more attractive. Down-to-earth, funny, and even sweet. He was also a good person, a smart and desirable guy that was a great catch by most women's standards.

There was a knock on the door and I snapped out of my thoughts. The door swung open before I could respond and Hay stuck his head around the corner and smiled.

"Ready, Fiona?"

"Yes, yes. Come in, Hay." I gestured to the chair that was on the opposite side of the desk and motioned for him to sit down. With his tight t-shirt accentuating his muscular chest and strong biceps, I almost forgot why he was here.
Focus, Fiona. The play? That's why he's here.

"What do you think of the final week of rehearsals? I think everything's coming along great," Hay said. "However, it's what the director thinks that really matters, isn't it?" He smiled and his eyes twinkled when he said that, making me bite back a smile. He knew how his charm affected me, and it was both amusing and of course, sexy. Everything Hayworth James did, seemed sexy to me.

"It's really shaped up."

"On that third song in the first act I think it would be more powerful for you to perform it to the right side of the stage. Balance things out. We seem to have gone left far more, I fear. I'm not sure how I didn't notice it earlier."

"You've noticed things that most people wouldn't. Don't worry about it. I'll go to the left for that song. Did you tell the guys or do you want me to tell them?"

"I meet with them first thing tomorrow," I said.

"No problem. We're going out for some beers tonight. I won't mention a thing though."

"That's nice."

"What do you mean?" Hay asked, looking at me curiously.

"That you all get along.   It makes a huge difference," she replied.

"It does. You make the biggest difference between success and mediocre for this production though, Fi."

"Thanks," I said.   We then kept staring at each other and it was clear that the big desk in between them wasn't big enough. The tension in the air between us was so thick, you could cut it with a knife. I wanted to reach over the desk, grab his shirt and tear it off so I could lick his chest and run my tongue all over it down to his large bulge in his jeans. Ever since our first meeting in my office, I couldn't help wonder what it would be like to have him fill me with it.

I must have been apparent with my desires because suddenly Hay began to act nervous, looking around at the office and hesitant to look at me again. He ran his fingers through his hair, which had grown longer to fit the Tristan role better, and breathed in.

I observed Hay and wondered what it was that had just changed in him. He clearly had gone from relaxed and casual to very nervous. But why?

"Fiona," Hay began. He looked at me, and I could see his jaw was pressed shut, trying to stop him from saying something he'd regret.

"What is it Hay?" I asked. Okay, I was worried by his sudden change in disposition.

"I wanted to thank you for giving me the opportunity to be in the musical. I never thought I could have been an actor or sing in front of a group before getting this role. You helped me see what I could do and while I definitely needed the job, it's more important to me than just a scholarship now. I just wanted you to know that."

I breathed a sigh of relief. "Aw Hay, it's always been inside of you. I feel lucky that I'm the one that's gotten to help you exploit your talents. You have real potential, you know. I'm still hoping that you'll think about going with us on a tour if we get everything organized for Rock Hard, Love Hard to go international."

"Finishing school's important to me…important to my parents too."

"I know and it's smart. I could never ask you not to, but when there's a will, there is a way," I said. I'd gotten up and walked around the desk to the side of Hay. My hand patted his shoulder and I continued talking. "Look, I have every confidence that you will rock this role and great things will happen for you as a result, Tristan…I mean Hay. I just know it."

"I'm glad you feel it. I don't want to screw anything up. Every person has worked so hard and I know there are going to be a lot of eyes on me. I've tried to prove myself more, knowing that people were thinking that some jock was walking into their turf – that I don't belong on stage any more than they belong on a football field."

"I never got that impression. Your personality is one that everyone seems to respond to," I said, smiling with my arms crossed. I was about one foot away from Hay and leaning against the edge of my desk, watching him as his insecurities were exposed. Oddly enough, it made him seem stronger than ever.

"I just don't want to screw anything up, Fi," he said honestly. "I know how much this means to you."

"You won't screw up, Hay," I said. I was absolutely confident about it too. "Plus, it's not me that should be worried about pleasing. It's the audience. I know you'll do that because you have something that far too few people do have."

"What's that?" Hay asked.

"A sense of pride in what you do. It makes all the difference."

Hay stood up and stood within inches of me, closing the gap between us. "But," he said, touching my arm softly and then his fingers were on my face, "it's because of you that I am here. You're amazing and I can't help wanting to be the best I can be for you, Fi. And it's not only that you're amazing and clearly a talented director; you're also the most beautiful person I've ever seen or met."

Then Hay moved in as close as he could and pressed his lips against mine, kissing gently. Then the urgency of his emotions and desires showed through and his tongue caressed mine, as he began passionately devouring my mouth. I wanted him to kiss me so badly I didn't push him away and my lips naturally responded, kissing him back. Hay kissed my eyes, my cheeks, and my the area close to my ear and whispered, "These last few weeks have been the best weeks of my life. I am so much in love with you, Fi."

Rock Hard Love Hard (Rock Hard Musical #1)

Those were the words that had snapped me out of the moment. I'd aggressively been avoiding hearing them from Michael…thinking he might say them. I never did anything or encouraged anything that would lead Hay to say them. "Hay, I can't. I'm with Michael and…"

Hay interrupted me by kissing me again. "You felt that, didn't you?"

I stared at him, not answering feeling suddenly very confused and torned. Hay continued talking. "You felt how it could be with us. I know you're with Michael and he's the producer of this musical, maybe even your mentor. That's cool, but do you love him? Or, are you one of his pet projects. I know his reputation and the distance he'll go for something he wants to possess. He's smooth and slick, and has gone through so many women."

"I hardly think…" I began, but Hay put his finger up to my lips so he could continue what he was saying. He had to get it out and release the tension of all the emotions he had pent up inside.

"His tastes in women are well known, Fiona, and I know you are not like that. I can tell by everything you say, everything you do. You're more than just a play thing for a rich man, you know. You deserve to be the center of the universe for any lucky man who gets to have you. I'm not wealthy, I'm still finishing school, but I do have the means to make you the center of my universe. I love you. Nothing else matters."

"It's not that simple," I said, shocked to find myself having this conversation. Why haven't I seen it coming. Wasn't Hay with Poppy?

"Yes, it is that simple, Fi. You wrote the part of Tristan for a reason. It's a beautiful role that shows the complexity of a young man who has goals and ambitions; and he finds himself rising up to become an icon, but learn a whole lot about himself along the way. It's genius because you're genius. It makes me upset that you have to prostitute yourself and sleep with a man like *him* in order to be taken seriously as a writer and director of a phenomenal musical. It shouldn't have to be that way."

I looked at Hay and my first instinct was to slap him for saying such a thing. Prostitute myself? How dare he? That was a ballsy thing to say for sure. Before my hand could extend out and deliver a stinging slap across his face I stopped myself. If I was to be honest, I knew that there was truth in what Hay had said. Did people see me that way? If they did, I didn't understand how I couldn't have seen it. I was always so conscious of using nothing more than my hard work and determination every day at work, never throwing out any clout cards by tossing Michael's name into it. There was no denying that he'd done a lot to help me with the production and it wouldn't exist without him, but it was more involved than being a prostitute.

"Thank you for your input, Hay. Now if you don't mind, I have to get going," I said. I stared at him and he sighed and walked out the door. I waited for a minute to make sure he was gone and then I left, making my way to the car and home to get ready for the benefit. Suddenly I was looking forward to it even less than I had before.

CHAPTER 14

The words that Hay had said were bugging me more than I cared for. I shouldn't care what he thought, but they had stung. I had to get them out of her mind before the night though. Tonight, her focus was on Michael, his parents, and their benefit. It was so challenging though.

Wearing a black cocktail dress I got ready, deciding to put my hair up that evening in a French roll with a beautiful gemmed butterfly clip to hold it in place. I assessed myself, wanting to dress to impress and not look too sexy. *Damn that Hay*. He has me evaluating what I'm wearing and how I look in it.

Michael came up behind me and wrapped his arms around my waist, pressing against my back. I could feel his hard-on as he did that. It pressed into the small of my back.

"We have a few minutes. Interested in doing anything fun before the benefit?" Michael asked.

I turned around and looked at him, smiling in appreciation for the offer, but I was not interested in anything like that now. "Why don't we wait? It'll give you motivation to not stay out too late," I said.

"I like the way you think, you dirty little girl," Michael said.

I wanted to tell him to stop saying things like that, but I just let it slide. It wasn't the time to start anything. I was distracted enough as it was so I just accepted his words and put the final touches on my make-up. Then it was time to go.

"The lobby called. The car is downstairs."

Rock Hard Love Hard (Rock Hard Musical #1)

"Are your parents in it?" I asked.

"Oh no. We'll only be seeing them at the benefit."

"How about tomorrow?" I asked, feeling a bit of panic. I haven't scheduled out time for entertaining them because I was already strapped for time for the musical.

"No, they'll be flying out in the morning to their next destination, whatever that is."

"You don't know?"

"No, I'm busy. They're busy. We don't bother with details like that. They're highly irrelevant."

I couldn't help but reflect on how important Hay's parents were to him and the fact that although he was a great distance away, he'd do anything for them if he could. So different than Michael.

"I see. Well, let's get going then," I said.

The two went downstairs and made their way to the hall where the benefit was taking place. The ride was casual and I asked as much information as I could about Michael's parents so I'd have something interesting to say…or so I hoped.

When I walked into the hall I couldn't help but be impressed at how well organized it was for their charity cause. There was a children's choir singing up front and it was so sweet and touching, really reminding everyone of what their cause was and how important it was to them.

Michael's parents must have eagerly been awaiting his arrival because the second that he and I walked into the room they were there.

"Michael, darling," his mother said.

Rock Hard Love Hard (Rock Hard Musical #1)

"Hello mother," he said, kissing her on the cheek. It was very formal and awkward looking to Fiona. More show on both their parts than genuine love for each other.

"Dale and Regina Bailey, this is Fiona Wilde," Michael said, turning to me and smiling at me. His smile was also guarded to me, but I guessed that was just how their family interacted. What a shame.

"Hello, it's a pleasure to meet you both," I said, extending my hand.

"The phenom from the musical," Dale said. "No wonder why Michael is so aggressively pursuing your musical going international."

"That's very flattering," I said, smiling. I instantly liked Michael's dad and he was merry and lively, not at all stuffy the way Michael's mother appeared to be.

Regina cleared her throat. "Dale, would you go and get us all some champagne," she said.

"Yes dear," he said.

After Dale was gone, Regina began to ask me a ton of questions about my past, what my current plans were, and the musical. She was very kind and sweet, easy to open up to, but I couldn't help but think she was subtly trying to find out if I was a gold digger. Apparently it was uncommon for Michael to even introduce a woman in his life to them, but he had. I felt special.

I found myself making her way around the room, always next to Michael or close to his watchful eye, and was actually thankful when it was time for me to play the piano. It would give me a bit of space.

When my name was called, along with a plug for Rock Hard, Love Hard, I went up and sat down, instantly drifting away to my imagined paradise, which is what often happened when I played. It was by far the most relaxing thing I could do, even more so than exercise. When I finished my number, Metamorphoses V by Phillip Glass, everyone stood and clapped. I stood up and bowed, then walked off the stage, where Michael and his father were waiting. His mother was on the stage, ready to announce what was happening next.

"That was splendid, darling," Michael said, kissing my cheek.

"Most lovely. You are a very talented young lady," Dale said. Then he drank down his champagne and took off to find a waiter for another glass.

"What do you say we get out of here?" Michael asked huskily.

"Sounds good," I said. I was all too happy to leave, having had enough of the event tonight. With all the hours of rehearsals and social events, I was feeling exhausted and

Kailin Gow

that's why I couldn't shake the nagging thoughts that something wasn't adding up.

Once we got back home, Michael was all over me. As much as I wanted him just as much, I was admittedly a bit exhausted. Slumping into bed for a great night's sleep sounded absolutely inviting above anything else.

I went into the room and began to unzip the back of my dress. It slid down to the ground as Michael came up behind me and began to fastening something around my neck. It was a necklace and after he fastened it he told me to go look in the mirror. I walked over and stared at it.

"It's beautiful, Michael. So unique," I said, admiring the funky kitschy necklace. It had pave-encrusted gems and diamonds on the collar of it.

"I'm glad you like it. It's more than a necklace, you know."

Rock Hard Love Hard (Rock Hard Musical #1)

"What do you mean?" I asked, hoping it wasn't some sign of something more intimate. I wasn't prepared for another one of those encounters today.

"It's a statement to everyone who knows what a necklace like that means," Michael continued.

"And it means what?" I asked again, wondering why he wasn't just getting to the point. That was unlike him.

"It means you're mine."

I turned around and smiled, seeing the possessive side of him show through. It was a beautiful necklace though. Then he did something that surprised me. He clicked a small diamond chain to one of the loops at the bottom of the collar and then took a few steps back and started to gently pull on it, making me walk toward him.

He leaned in and kissed me on the mouth hard, sliding his tongue in and not letting go. When he paused he looked into my eyes and spoke his heart. "Masters give their prize subs collars. It's a high honor and status amongst subs. Does that excite you?"

My jaw dropped open, not expecting him to say that. Suddenly I realized that there was no love in Michael for me. I was an object, a play thing first and foremost. "Is that what I am to you, Michael? Your sub? Your object that submits to your every desire or demand?" I was shaking now, trying to avoid the anger that was surging through me. I felt embarrassed and ashamed that I'd dare imagine more with him – thoughts of a real future together as a good couple, two people meant to be together.

Michael smiled and crossed his arms, still holding onto the diamond chain that connected us. "Well, sort of, if you want to be technical about it," he said.

Clearly flabbergasted, I could not even talk. Michael took it as an opportunity to express exactly what he was thinking. "That's what you and I do, Fi. We haven't been kinky thus far because you are so new to this. You must be broken in slowly, like a wild mustang. We've been very vanilla thus far and I've been very patient about it, but it's time to move on. You're ready and I'll guide you there."

"Guide me there?" I finally managed to spit out.

"Don't get me wrong," Michael said, turning a bit more serious. "You've been worth the wait, but I have needs that are more, shall we say aggressive, than what we've done. You're ready for more and I'm going to take you to places that test the limits of your mind and the intense pleasure of your sexuality."

Michael tried to kiss me again, but I stepped back and took the small diamond rope out of his hands, holding onto it. "So that's all I am to you?" she repeated. "Some kind of play thing that you're waiting to open up and put your hands all over?"

Seeing that his offer of the collar wasn't going where he expected it would, Michael began to explain himself. "It's not like that," he said, rubbing his hand on my hair. I shook her head, not accepting his touch. "Fiona, you're more to me than a play thing. If that's all you were we wouldn't be living together. I wouldn't have made sure you got to direct and see your musical through either. I enjoy your company very much."

"Like a roommate?" I asked bitterly. Then I added, "A friend with benefits."

"More than that, Fiona. For God's sake. I enjoy talking to you and you are exceptional at events that we attend together. You're beautiful, warm, and inviting. And yes, I enjoy fucking you too. That's a compliment." Now Michael was clearly annoyed, feeling it was beneath him to have to explain himself; especially to his sub.

Rock Hard Love Hard (Rock Hard Musical #1)

I looked up at the ceiling and cursed under my breath. How could I have been so stupid. I mumbled, "Damn, Hay was right."

"Hay? What does Hay have to do with this conversation?" he asked. He was immediately suspicious and clearly irked by the mention of the name.

I quickly realized that I may have just gotten Hay into trouble and that was not my intent. I looked at Michael and reached out the diamond rope to him, offering to give it back. "Nothing. I meant, 'hey, it's alright.' Now, Master, what's next?" I cringed at how idiotic it all sounded and hoped my face didn't give it away. I was not happy and I was not in the mood, but I also knew full well that Michael would just stomp out Hay in a second if he perceived him to be a threat. It was actually ridiculous when you thought about it. He was not wealthy, he was a college student, and he wasn't even twenty-one years old yet. What type of threat was that to a man of Michael's age and stature?

To show that I meant what I said, I leaned in and kissed Michael passionately on the lips, using my tongue to open his mouth wider and to tangle with his. He groaned as I reached down a hand and began running my fingers along his bulge. When I broke off the kiss, he was breathing heavy. I kissed his ear and whispered, "Thank you for the beautiful necklace. I can't wait to see where it takes me when I have it on."

Michael smiled, clearly pleased with his victory and ready to show his sub just what was expected of me. He yanked down on the chain. "On your knees now." His voice was eerily quiet, but authoritative. I dropped down to my knees and stared up at Michael, waiting for my next command.

"Unzip my pants now and please me."

"Yes," Fiona whispered. "With pleasure."

"Silence," Michael growled.

Rock Hard Love Hard (Rock Hard Musical #1)

I did as I was told and unzipped Michael's pants. As soon as it was unzipped, his hard engorged cock sprung out of them into my hands. I stroke it, and placed my lips on it. I began teasing him by licking him with my tongue and exploring his full length with my lips, before taking him fully into my mouth. Oh, he was delicious, and I began sucking hard on him, while using my tongue to flick his tip.

"Fuck, Fi, that is good," Michael said. "I knew you were a natural pleaser."

His words encouraged me to please him more so I sucked him in and out of my mouth, occasionally running my teeth along his length, causing him to groan. Michael closed his eyes, and grabbed my hair, pulling me closer to him so I could take him in deeper. Then he began pumping back and forth as hard as he could, holding my hair so my back was arched while he did it. Through his silence everything that needed to be said was said. He was enjoying me as his sub wearing the collar and the feeling complete dominance over me. And to be honest, although the sub thing was something that I was uncomfortable with at first, I was getting highly aroused by it. When he released my hair and was about to come, I cried, "Please come in me now. Please I need…"

"Silence. No begging," Michael said before he pulled me up, turned me behind, and plunged into me with a fury that rocked me up the wall. He pumped and pumped until we both climaxed, crying out each other's names.

I fell into his arms in complete exhaustion and relaxation, as he cried his pleasure into my hair. "You're mine Fiona. Mine. No other man can touch you or I'll kill him or you both."

CHAPTER 15

Full dress rehearsals are an imperative part of preparing for any production's opening night and run. It's where the kinks get worked out of the system, everything is finessed, and you can truly see how the hard work of everyone has paid off. The entire week before opening day was to be filled with one complete dress rehearsal a night, followed by re-enacting specific sections that were a bit weak or lacking in something.

It was huge and I was relying on everyone to do their part to the best of their abilities. Likewise, they were also relying on me to do what I must to ensure that my artistic eye was capturing the essence of all their individual actions, as well as those they did as a troupe.

After that night in my office, Hay and I had been nothing short of professional with each other. We both chose to forget the entire incident had happened. It was good and I was very relieved that no one in the cast and crew seemed to realize that we'd had such an 'interesting' discussion. Knowing that Hay's words had been right was something that I couldn't accept yet. It wasn't the right time. Until I had a plan, I'd just do what I had to do and at that time, it was getting the musical set.

"Where's Hay?" I asked, looking at my actors up on the stage.

"He's not here yet, I don't think," Pittsburgh said.

"Not here? Has anyone heard from him? I wonder why he's running late." I grabbed my cell phone from the clip and looked to see if I'd missed a message. I hadn't.

"What should we do?" Sasha/Poppy asked. I looked at her and a thought hit me. Had something happened between those two? Something to make Hay decide not to show up. I had to find out.

"Do you have a minute, Poppy?" I asked, smiling and trying to show that it was casual. I could feel all eyes on us at the theater after I asked.

"Sure," she said, looking at me oddly. We went to the corner of the stage, just behind one of the long black curtains that hid all the commotion that happened behind the scenes.

"I have to be blunt here. Sorry in advance for that," I began. "I need to make sure that nothing happened with you and Hay off the set that would make him not show up today."

"Seriously? You think I'd jeopardize my opportunity by doing that?" Poppy began. "I can assure you, Miss Wilde, I've come too far and done too much work to do that. I don't know where he is, but if I find him…"

"You don't need to find him. I just had to check. We're going to start rehearsals without him. His understudy will have to step in until he shows up. You can guide him through everything," I said.

Poppy nodded and was off, back on stage, and calling over the understudy.

I went out into the theater to sit in a chair in the first row and observe everything from the audience's perspective. I watched everyone do their part and everyone was doing a great job for the most part, but it was so distracting not seeing Hay up there as Tristan. His understudy was decent, but he was no Hay when it came to the role. Hay brought something special to the role that couldn't be replaced.

The entire rehearsal had ended up well, all things considered, but Hay had not shown up. Something must have happened, I know because Hay would not abandon the musical like that. I had to go find him and figure out what was going on. I called it a wrap after the dress rehearsal.

On the way out of the theater I saw Jerome and Ferro standing there. They were talking casually and each on their phones, checking their text messages.

"Hey, do you guys have finals coming up?" I asked.

"Not for a few weeks," Ferro said.

"Okay. Do either of you have Hay in any classes?"

"Nope," Jerome said.

"I was just wondering if he was sick."

"No idea."

"Okay, thanks guys. I'll see you tomorrow," I said. I walked out to my car and made my way over to Hay's apartment, hoping I'd find him there. She had a sinking feeling in the pit of her stomach and she didn't like it. She felt so nervous and on edge. Not once did it cross her mind that she couldn't count on Hay to be there, doing what he'd done so dedicatedly for the past month and a half.

When I pulled into the apartment complex I saw that Hay's car was in the parking lot. That was a relief. But then again, what the hell? If he was at the apartment there was no reason for him to not have shown up to practice or at least called to say why he couldn't make it.

I walked up the stairs to Hay's second floor apartment and began to knock on the door, softly at first. I pressed my ear against it and couldn't hear anything. I knocked louder, thinking maybe he was sick in bed and just couldn't hear me.

"Hay! Hay, it's Fiona. Are you in there?"

Rock Hard Love Hard (Rock Hard Musical #1)

Still no answer.

I heard a door open up from behind her and a college girl whose hair was up in a bun on her head and had a pencil in her mouth was staring at her. "He's clearly not there. Do you mind? I'm trying to get a project done here."

"Sorry. When's the last time you saw Hay?"

"You mean the playboy? Oh, that's his name. No clue. I don't really pay attention to everything that happens over there," she said.

"Okay, thank you," I said. The girl shut her door and I reached into her purse and wrote a note, asking Hay to call me the second he got it. I slid it under the door and went home.

That night I was cranky and distracted. When Michael asked why, I lied and just said that I had a headache. I went to bed and lied there, thinking about where Hay could be and what was going on. When Michael came to bed I pretended to be sleeping so I wouldn't have to talk or risk taking any of his advances that night. I was not in the mood. Finally I did drift off to sleep, resolved to the fact that Hay would be back at rehearsal the next day. Hopefully.

The next day came quickly and once again, Hay did not show up for rehearsals. It was so aggravating to me because I didn't know whether to be worried, to tell the understudy to be prepared for a marathon of preparation, or to just be mad that Hay was being an asshole. No one from the cast had seen him anywhere or was able to get a hold of him either. I had everyone looking.

This night, after rehearsals, I decided to take a walk and enjoy the nice day. Maybe it would give me some clarity or a new idea on where to find Hay or where he was at. I looked up and saw a flyer on a billboard outside, talking about how the football team was doing some sort of fundraiser for charity. That was it. I would go talk to

Rock Hard Love Hard (Rock Hard Musical #1)

Hay's coach. The man had always been important to Hay and was a real mentor to him. In fact, he was the one who had brought Hay to me that day for auditions.

I walked through the field house, making my way to the location of the football coach's office. I rolled my eyes at some of the cat calls I got as I crossed the gym floor, thinking that those boys needed something better to do – like concentrate on their training.

I knocked on the door frame because it was open and the coach looked up. "Excuse me, I was wondering if you've seen Hay James at all?" I asked.

"Why are you looking for him?" the coach asked.

"I'm Fiona Wilde, the director for the musical he's cast in. He hasn't show up to rehearsal for two days. I'm trying to find him."

"That doesn't sound like Hay," the coach said.

"I didn't think so either, but I have no idea where he is. No one has found him."

"Did you check his house?"

"I did," I said. "So, no ideas?"

"None at all, but it must have been something urgent if he just ditched without a call. Just not like him. I'll keep an eye out and call his parents to check."

"Thank you," I said. "Here's my card. Would you mind letting me know that he's okay if you get word?"

"Not at all."

"Thanks." I left and now I was definitely worried more than anything else about Hay. His disappearing act wasn't typical. Did something happen to him? I had no idea where to look. Within ten minutes, the coach had already called me on my cell phone and said that Hay's parents hadn't seen him and couldn't get him to answer on his cell phone either.

I decided to call the police department, but they told me I couldn't file a missing person's report. That was something that his parents or a family member would have to do. I didn't want to scare his parents by asking them to do that. I'd just have to figure something out.

That night, I went home and drew a hot bath. I opened up a bottle of red wine and poured myelf a glass as I slipped into the hot steaming tub with fragrant lavender bubbles. It felt so good.

My mind was swirling and I was devastated. None of this made sense and no matter how hard I tried, I couldn't figure out how to grasp it. I was absolutely worried about Hay and if he was well. Selfishly, I was also worried about all the hard work of her musical. I knew that may seem cold, but I'd given my all to that production and I knew that it just wouldn't be the same quality with another Tristan.

"Fiona, where are you?" Michael called out.

I didn't want to answer. He was home earlier than I'd thought he would be. I'd just wanted to be alone and sulk in my misery.

Michael walked into the bathroom and looked at her.

"Oh honey, are you alright?"

"I can't find him. No one can find him," I said.

"Hay, you mean?"

"Yes, Hay," I said.

"Maybe it was just too much for him. I'm sorry," Michael said.

"Why wouldn't he talk to me then? That makes no sense. It's not like him."

"You only know him professionally. Perhaps he's not really that great of a person deep down. You're so good, always expecting the best in everyone. Maybe he just couldn't live up to the bill."

I didn't answer. I just turned away and stared at the wall, drinking down the rest of my glass of wine. Michael came up behind me and began to massage my shoulders in the tub. It felt good.

"You're so tense. I'll take care of you," Michael said.

I nodded my head yes, but couldn't talk. A tear ran down my cheek. After my bath had gone cold I got out of the tub and Michael dried me off and guided me to the bedroom, where he laid me under the soft sheets and then crawled in next to me, hugging me and giving me comfort.

For the next two days, I didn't get out of my bed for anything more than what I had to. Michael had offered to go and look over rehearsals, saying he was at fault for not being there enough. Then he said he was sorry and began to kiss me all over my body, making sweet and tender love to me. I responded back and it felt good, but the second it was over, the feelings of despair returned.

The only thing that had really proven to be good about the past days was the fact of how Michael showed that he really did care about me and my well-being emotionally too. Perhaps I was more than just the sub, the piece of arm candy that he was proud to show off. Perhaps he really did love me, as I thought I had imagined him saying.

CHAPTER 16

After two days of self-pity and emotional collapse, I decided it was time to get back to work. There was only one more rehearsal and then it was opening day. I had to get my act together and accept that Hay was gone, regardless of the reason, and move on. The entire cast and crew were relying on me, Michael had invested a great deal of time, energy, and expense, and as they say in the business: the show must go on.

I walked into the theater, almost feeling like a stranger there despite all of the time I'd spent in there over the past months. Everyone looked at me and waved, glad to hear that my flu bug had gone away. I smiled. That Michael was clever, not letting anyone know that I had a massive melt down. I'd have to thank him later.

As I called out the orders and caught up with the understudy before the run through began, I saw Hay walk into the theater and casually stroll up on stage. He was acting so nonchalant, like nothing was out of the ordinary.

I could not believe my eyes. I couldn't believe he was back. Just like that.

When I saw that he clearly didn't care about how he'd put everyone in such a compromising position this past week I was instantly furious.

"Hay, to my office…now!" That was all I said and I stormed off the set. Hay looked at everyone else and then followed me. He saw that none of them were smiling either, except for his understudy.

"What's wrong?" Hay asked. He looked genuinely confused and that made me even more pissed off.

Rock Hard Love Hard (Rock Hard Musical #1)

"What's wrong? You just abandon us on opening week and stroll in here like you can do whatever you want. I expected more of you. I thought you were different. I thought this was important to you," I spat out.

"I'm sorry. I'm not sure what to say. I know I had to leave at the last minute, but I left a message with the janitor to put on your desk explaining everything. It was urgent."

"I didn't get any message," I said. I wanted to let down my guard a bit, but was hesitant to do so. Hay still had some serious explaining to do. "What was so urgent?"

"Well, with your talk of taking the show internationally possibly, I decided to get an agent. It was easier than I thought it would be. Honestly, I had assumed it would take a half a year or so...more like the stories I hear from others. Only it didn't."

"And," I said, tapping my fingers on my folded arms.

"He called with an urgent audition. I had to take a red eye to Vegas and they kept me there for all these days, doing pictures, film takes, readings, etc."

"For what part?"

"That's the weird thing. I never really met with someone for a standard audition, or what I thought would be one, until just last night. I hadn't had a great feeling about things, but the audition made me think that I was definitely not going to be getting any role any time too soon."

"Why?"

"It was out in the middle of the desert, for one thing. Not even at a studio, but at a back room to some bar out there. I could hear slots going off in another room and it wasn't a very nice looking place."

Rock Hard Love Hard (Rock Hard Musical #1)

"Really? That sounds odd."

Hay shrugged his shoulders. "It was odd. The guy holding the auditions was one creepy looking bastard too. He reminded me of a mobster or some shifty character from a movie. Not a producer or casting agent, that's for sure."

"Did you call your agent? What did they say?"

"He said it was fine. Just to be patient and not blow the opportunity. Even if I didn't get the role it would be good exposure and practice for future auditions."

"I guess that makes sense," I said.

"Well, the exposure ended up being a bit more than I would have bargained for, suffice it say."

"What do you mean?"

"I mean he asked me to strip and put my hands up. Then his phone rang and he turned around and talked for a few minutes. I didn't do anything because I was curious to see why I'd need to do that. I didn't know if this was actually porn or something like that. Anyway, he turned back around and told me there's been a change of plans and I didn't have to do anything. He had to wait for further instructions from his boss before doing anything else."

"And that was it?" I asked, looking incredulously at him.

"That was it," Hay said. "I was back here on the red eye. Spent all day catching up on homework and getting ready for tonight." Then he looked at me and said, "I'm sorry. I had no idea I was leaving you hanging. I thought I'd covered everything, Fi."

"That's okay. I'm just glad you're back, and you're alright. That sounds like a really suspicious audition. Did the guy give you his business card?"

Rock Hard Love Hard (Rock Hard Musical #1)

"No, no card. He said my agent had it and that he'd be in touch."

"Strange. Did you get a good look at him?"

"Not really. The lighting wasn't great and he had shades and a hat on the entire time. The only thing recognizable about him was the tattoo on his forearm. It was a scorpion. The thing was huge and elaborate."

That caught my attention. I knew of one person with a scorpion tattoo on his forearm and he wasn't a director or casting agent. He was a lackey thug drug dealer from Vegas; someone that Michael happened to know and that he used to help him out in certain situations. Why would this guy be out in the middle of the desert with Hay? I didn't know, but I'd have to think about that later. Right now, it was time for rehearsal.

"I really am glad you're back, Hay. We have a lot to do. This is the last rehearsal before opening night tomorrow. Go get changed and I'll let your understudy know you'll still be opening up, okay?"

"Okay," Hay said. He ran out of my office and into the changing room, leaving me standing in my office, a little shaken, but also relieved.

I realized that I had no idea of the lengths that Michael would go to when it came to getting what he wanted. He was linked to what happened. I was positive about it. Furthermore, he'd used it as an opportunity to show me that he really loved me and was supportive – that he was there for me. It had been crafty, but it was a low thing to do. Really slimy. Then again, I couldn't just assume that it was Michael. Nothing had happened to Hay after all.

After a brilliant rehearsal I felt back to my old self. Hay hadn't missed a beat and was spot on with everything, making me feel considerably more relaxed than what I had been. Yes, it was going to work out great after all.

Rock Hard Love Hard (Rock Hard Musical #1)

That night, I was so excited when I got home, but I still had my suspicions about Michael and what he'd done. I heard him in the shower, getting ready for a business meeting that night with some guys he was forming a new venture with, and I happened to walk past his telephone.

Knowing it was wrong, but not really caring, I picked it up and began to look through his call history, hoping I didn't see anything suspicious…anything to and from Vegas in the past few days. Such was not the case though. There were about five calls to Vegas, all the way through last night.

"Oh Michael, why?" I whispered, my heart dropping.

"Why what?" he asked, standing there staring at me with an odd look on his face. I realized I was holding his phone and I couldn't hide the guilt on my face.

"Sorry, I thought it was mine. I really should get a case on mine so I can tell it from yours," I said.

"Yes, you really should."

"You must have business going on in Las Vegas, huh?"

Michael stared at me, as if trying to read my thoughts. Then he broke out into a smile. "Shoot, you ruined the surprise."

"What surprise?"

"After the run at the theater, I'm planning an extra special and fun trip to Vegas for us. I didn't want you to know."

"Oh, I'm sorry," I said. I went up and hugged Michael tightly before kissing him. I wanted him to believe I was showing my appreciation, and trying to hide my burning face, which clearly showed I was frazzled about being busted with his phone and that I didn't believe what he said. However, I knew I'd be going to Vegas now for that surprise. There was no way he'd change that. "I'm sure it'll be great and I definitely know you'll have lots of surprises in store for me," I said.

"Oh yeah?" he asked.

"Naturally, Michael Bailey is a man who can pull off surprising things like no one else I've ever met." I nuzzled his ear with my lips. "I can't wait to find out what surprises you have for me. I'm already wet thinking of it." I softly and slowly traced the corner of his mouth with my tongue, as he opened his mouth to take it in and kissed me hard.

"I like it when you say those types of things to me, Fiona. It turns me on," he said huskily.

"Me too," I replied. I realized how good I'd gotten at acting submissive to him. I had no idea of what my future with Michael would be, but for now, I had to please him the best I can in order to keep the show going and maybe even to keep Hay safe.

"Well, I'll see you later," Michael said, kissing me quickly on the lips. "I might be late. Don't wait up too late, okay?"

"Okay," I said.

When he left, I blew out a big breath of relief, and looked down at my hand. They could not stop shaking.

CHAPTER 17

The morning of opening day had come and I was so excited about the musical finally taking place that I couldn't stop talking about it as I ate breakfast with Michael.

I was excited and nervous to see how it all turned out, but also relaxed. I knew I'd put in the time and did absolutely everything possible that I could do to ensure that the musical was a success from my point of view. I couldn't make the audience respond positively, but I'd put as much as I could in place as I could from their perspective to draw them in and instantly fall in love with the Granite Gods and Rock Hard, Love Hard.

"I'm so relieved to have Hay playing Tristan again," I said. "He really is a difference maker for the entire thing. He's the chemistry, the star that everyone gravitates toward."

"Did you say you put him back in? After he left you an emotional mess for all those days?" Michael asked, setting down the fork that he'd been using to eat his eggs Benedict.

"Yes, it made the most sense and he explained everything," I said.

Michael didn't bother asking what the explanation was. He just continued on. "He's a college kid, a jock at heart, and probably so cocky he thought he could just do what he wanted without any consequences."

"Weren't you a college student and a jock at one point?"

"But at an Ivy League College, not USC."

Rock Hard Love Hard (Rock Hard Musical #1)

"Seriously?" I asked. Then I knew it wasn't the time to get into an argument about it. I had too much to do and Hay was my choice regardless of what Michael said. I'd decided that it wasn't worth it to confront him about what happened and his suspected role in it. What good would it do? All I had to do was focus on the next two weeks and having them be an amazing success, one that would ensure that the musical did go international, with or without Michael's help.

"Well, I just hope he doesn't leave you hanging again. It was really hard watching you in that condition," Michael said. "I need my girlfriends to be strong."

"Except when you want them to be submissive," I said.

Michael laughed, seeming to be amused by my quirky sarcasm. "Exactly. Well, I've got to get going. I'm meeting you here at six to leave for the theater, right?"

"Yes, six," I said.

Michael kissed her forehead and walked out of the small breakfast nook area and into his office so he could grab his briefcase, suit jacket, and phone. Then he was gone.

I left shortly after him, going to the theater and going through the entire checklist with the stage manager. Everything was set and in place. Next it was off to get my hair done and a manicure and pedicure. Then I had to be back to the theater by 3 p.m. for a quick meeting with the entire cast and crew. Then it was home to get ready and back to the theater for the most exciting day of my life. I could not wait.

* * *

Walking into the theater with Michael was so exciting. There was a small press room where I'd answer some questions about the musical, plus its cast and crew for the critics, and then they'd be sitting in the audience watching the musical unfold. I made sure they'd had the best seats. I had also flown in Hay's parents as a surprise for him too. They deserved to see how talented their son was and the product of his hard work and efforts. His entire football team was also there; ready to see him in a different kind of action.

After handing out the press packets and ensuring I thanked all fifteen critics there personally for coming to the musical, I made my way into the theater, watching it fill up with people. I quickly introduced myself to Hay's parents, who were so kind and lovely. They smiled at me and I could see a bit of each of them in their son. You could how proud they were proud of Hay, which also made me swell u with pride for him.

Then I made my way backstage and found a frantic and chaotic scene back there, unlike the happy calmness of the theater and the guests waiting to enjoy the play. The chaos was a mix of busy activity and pre-show jitters, but it made me feel so alive and absolutely great. Everyone was hustling around, the stage manager was barking out orders, and the costume staff was checking and double checking that everything fit perfectly and there wouldn't be any wardrobe malfunctions.

Finally it was time for the lights to dim. I peeked out around the curtain and saw Michael in the audience. He was looking off to the right of me and waving with a sultry smile on his face. I looked in the direction of his glance and saw that it was Poppy who played Sasha, on the receiving end of it. *I wonder*, I thought. *Oh well, it doesn't really matter.*

The stage went dark and everyone who was in the first scene of act one got into place on the stage and then the lights went on and the audience was transported into an intense experience, combining youth, music, and life's lessons into one experience. I stared, frozen in place, watching it all unfold. After the first minute, I finally let my breath go. I'd done all I could and now it was out of my hands and in the hands of the actors, audience, and critics.

Rock Hard Love Hard (Rock Hard Musical #1)

Before I knew it, two hours had gone by and I watched as the cast took their bows and many standing ovations. A beautiful dozen of giant red roses with tips dipped in black were given to Sasha, the female lead, and she bowed gracefully, showing that she truly had lived that role like it was her real life. She was a good actress and deserved it. I was happy for her.

Hay, just like I'd known he would, got so much applause, whistles, and cheers. He'd transported everyone right into his life as Tristan, leaving the audience cheering for him and feeling like they knew him. I couldn't have been more pleased.

Then Hay and the entire cast turned to me and called me over. *This is it,* I thought. *Time to take my bow.*

When I walked out and they handed me a giant bouquet of flowers, white and red mixed together, and with glittery music notes scattered into them I smiled, smelling their intoxicating fragrance. It wasn't as intoxicating as the feeling of being appreciated and respected as a professional in that moment though. That was priceless and I would savor it forever. If that was the only applause I ever got, it would be enough for me.

Afterward, the lights all came on and the cast went out to talk with people in the theater as they were living. They'd been instructed to do so because it was part of making them absolutely real to the audience. It brought the Granite Gods to life in real life, not just theatrical life.

I stood by Michael's side and we talked with many people, building the connections that would take the musical the distance, and also answering questions from the press. Through the corner of my eye, I could see Hay talking with his parents and football friends, laughing and having a great time. Women kept coming up to him and some of the younger ones were actually asking him to sign the playbill. He did so, smiling at each of them and making them feel like they were the only person in the world. It was a look that I had received from Hay and absolutely loved. She'd melted right into those dreamy blue eyes with the bright white all American smile.

After everyone had slowly trickled out and the crew began to make their way back stage to change and call it a night – a successful night at that – Hay called me over. He had his backpack and pulled something out from it. This had caught Michael's attention and he came over too, standing protectively behind me.

"Here. I thought you might like these," Hay said, ignoring Michael. Clearly the two were not impacted by each other's presence the same way. Hay handled Michael like a pro, but Michael on the other hand, puffed out his chest like a silver back gorilla showing its dominance.

"Thanks Hay," I said. I took the box and lifted off the lid and stared down at it. I began to laugh and a happy tear trickled down my cheeks. "It's perfect," I said. I walked over to Hay and hugged him tightly.

"What is that? Cream puffs?" Michael asked.

"Yes, cream puffs," I said.

"Well, I guess that this will pale in comparison to that," he added, pulling a long slender jewelry box out of his pocket.

At first, I cringe a bit, hoping he wasn't giving me one of his kinky things right here in front of Hay and the other cast members.

I opened it up slowly and stared down. It was a diamond bracelet in platinum with an emerald shaped starburst in the center. Truly exquisite.

"Thank you, Michael. It's lovely," I said.

"Well, are you ready?" Michael asked.

"Yes," I said. Then I turned to Hay. "Great job tonight"

Rock Hard Love Hard (Rock Hard Musical #1)

"Thanks. I'm nervous about the reviews, I'll admit. I've never been under such scrutiny before."

"I don't think you have anything to worry about," I said. "Don't you agree, Michael?"

Michael smiled, staring at Hay. "Of course not. You cast him brilliantly, dear."

By morning, the reviews were all out and I was in a reading frenzy, looking online at all of the websites where the critics worked at or owned. I was so nervous, trying to read slowly so I could absorb every word.

As she read each review, I couldn't have been more pleased. The only critical comment had to do with thinking that there was too much lighting in some of the musical numbers. That was not a big deal though and I disagreed with that assessment. No one, aside from one critic, noted it. I was also excited to see that #GraniteGods was trending in the local market.

For the next two weeks it was seven shows a week with Monday's off. Every night there was a packed house and the legend of the Granite Gods and Rock Hard, Love Hard grew. I had started to receive some calls about others interested in putting on a production of the show themselves, hoping to find out how much it would cost for rights to use her play and get her expertise, and Michael had been trying to finalize some lucrative deals, addressing all the various aspects of taking a large production on the road to various cities around the world. There were logistics, variations in stage size and arena size, and a slew of other things that went into it.

Finally, it was closing night of the show. There was a special celebration planned for the entire cast and crew at a local restaurant. Michael had arranged it all and was taking everyone out as his treat. He'd invested a considerable amount financially into the musical, and luckily, the hit had paid off. He was grateful and was treating everyone to a great evening at one of the poshest restaurants in town.

"I'd like to propose a toast to all of you and the success that has come with Rock Hard, Love Hard. It's exceeded all our expectations and great things are in store for it down the road. No matter what happens, you will always be the first ones we will consider to reprise the roles. No one can replace that," Michael said.

Everyone held their glasses up and smiled, calling out a cheers and drinking down the smooth crisp Kristal that was in their champagne flutes.

As it ended up, Hay was sitting next to me so that I was in between Michael and him. How that happened, I have no idea. It was arranged by hierarchy, and being the director next to the star and producer was the way it turned out. However, the tension was interesting and unavoidable.

Michael was clearly on edge with Hay there and used every opportunity he had to rub his position into play. "So Hay, what is it that you're studying in school again?"

"Architecture right now, but I am considering switching to the theater program. There are some scholarships I qualify for."

"Ah, a taste of success has caused you to switch gears. Acting and music, it's a tough industry to get into. That's for certain."

"True, but I'm always up for a good challenge," Hay retorted.

"Hay is very talented. It sounds like a great change if he wants to explore it. He can always pursue architecture down the road again if he'd prefer it, or things didn't work out," I interjected. Hay was there because of me, and although I cared for Michael, I didn't want him to make Hay feel inferior. It didn't matter that Michael was the head honcho at the moment, I wanted the musical and the celebration to end on a joyous and positive high note, not some kind of bawl.

"Yes, I suppose that is true. It's just hard for me to manage having the time to pursue something that is risky at best."

"Oh, have all your investments been that safe? Have you always been in control?" Hay asked Michael directly.

My jaw dropped and Michael retorted. I finally tuned out, not sure what to think. Hay had more balls than I thought. Not just another pretty face so it seemed. I excused myself to go to the restroom and then sat back down on the other side of the table, talking to a few cast members down there. I'd had enough of the two alpha men trying to stake a claim on me for that evening. I wanted to spend my time with my cast and crew, and I wanted to thank them for putting on the greatest show I could've ever envisioned.

Then I noticed Poppy slip over to the spot in between Michael and Hay where I was and she immediately went to town, oozing out her charm and making both Hay and Michael seem to forget that they couldn't stand each other. Instant jealousy flooded through me, which I haven't anticipated at all. I just didn't know why I was jealous and over whom.

After everyone ate and drank way too much, people started parting ways. Hay stood up and came over to say goodbye to me, smiling and saying goodbye in a slightly slurred voice. "Fiona," he said, his eyes half-closed and even a bit heated, "I'll be seeing you." He looked like he wanted to say more, but all he said was, "This has been great, and I'm sure you're happy with everything."

I grinned. How could I not keep from beaming. It was a dream come true having my musical produced and come to life in front of my eyes? But something deeply intense and unspoken in Hay's eyes that seemed to look into my soul made me hesitate. "I'm pretty happy with how the musical turned out. You were a big part of it." I reached out to hug him, and he responded by pulling me tight against his chest.

"Fiona, you made my dream come true. You've touched me more than anyone has. Working with you, being with you, had meant more than you'll ever know." He pulled back after looking deep into my eyes, his beautiful blue eyes so intense with emotions, his face torn with desire and desolation. My heart started racing, and all my animal lust for him, which I tried to keep bottled up during rehearsals, flooded my body.

"Hay," I said, still maintaining my director role as I saw Michael walk towards us. "You were perfect. More than you will ever know." Then Michael came over and touched my shoulders possessively before asking whether I was ready to go. I nodded yes, while he led me away from Hay, who had an unreadable expression on his face.

Michael turned to the few people remaining. "The tab is open. Enjoy the night and have some fun. Stay as long as you like." The three who made up the rest of Granite Gods, aside from Tristan, thanked him and smiled.

"What a fantastic night that was," I smiled, still on a high. *Aside from you and Hay acting out a testosterone war right in front of me that is.*

"It was nice. It's always good to make the people you rely on feel special, don't you think?"

"Yes," I said. I didn't consider my actors to be the little people as Michael had inferred it. They were passionate and dedicated professionals, whom I had formed incredible friendships with throughout the course of the musical. They were an important part of the team, as I was.

When we arrived home, and I was changing out of my dress, Michael came up from behind me and kissed my shoulders before wrapping his arms around my waist. "I cannot wait until tomorrow, Fiona. I have so much planned for us…been waiting for this play to be done so I can have you all to myself again." Michael's hands slipped under my bra, and his fingers began circling my nipples. It felt good…real good, and I arched my back towards his chest, leaning into him. He unclasped my bra and turned me around to face him. "It's such a turn on seeing you take control of an entire production like that, Fiona. Beautiful and bright. Damn sexy too." He bent his head down and his mouth was now sucking on my nipples, flicking his tongue over them until I was moaning.

"It will be nice to get away with you," I said, smiling. "But couldn't we do everything you've planned here?" Vegas had never been her kind of town, but it sure seemed to have Michael eager and excited. He must have had some very interesting things planned.

Michael pushed me down on the bed and removed his clothes. He was ready and definitely not waiting for Vegas to get it on. "Oh, I'm not leaving you unsatisfied tonight, Fiona, but I've got something special planned for Vegas, and I can't wait to spend the entire weekend training you on it." He smiled widely as he made his way down my breasts, stomach and thighs. His warm tongue found my core and as soon as he began aggressively licking me and then sucking my clit, I was on the brink of exploding. "Hold on," Michael commanded. He trailed his finger down the center of my body, leaving a shivering trail after his touch. His hand landed in between my legs and into me, further pushing me to the brink.

"Michael," I panted, "can I come now?"

"Not yet," he growled.

"But…"

He plunged into me and started rocking into me back and forth until he was crying out. "Now!" he shouted. "Now." Then we erupted at the same time, releasing all the pent up stress and excitement we've had the entire week of opening night. My body shook out all the tension, and by the time I subsided, and Michael kissed my brow, I felt like jelly before falling asleep in Michael's arms.

CHAPTER 18

Michael couldn't wipe the cheeky grin off his face the entire time he and I were in the car on the way to the private airport hangar where he kept his company jet, or on the jet for that manner. It was surprisingly arousing because it felt good to know that someone wanted you so badly that he had planned an entire weekend of activities just to spend that time with you.

"Where are we staying?" I asked.

"It's a surprise, but I'm sure you'll love it."

"I can't imagine not loving it. You have nothing but high standards and exceptional taste when it comes to where you choose to stay and eat," I said. "What are we going to do?"

"You'll find out. The surprises I have set for you are things you've never experienced before, but are sure to love. You're built for pleasure and pleasure you shall receive," Michael said.

Deciding to play dumb, I asked, "Oh…are we going on one of those helicopter adventures or something like that?"

"Helicopters are exciting, but I think you know what I am referring to."

"Gambling at the hundred dollar slots?" I asked. Now I couldn't help it. I started laughing, making Michael burst out into laughter too.

"Is there anything I can get you, Mr. Bailey?" his attendant asked.

I looked at her and could see the lust for him written all over her face. Given the chance, she would have made it to the mile high club with him, if she hadn't already. She glanced over at Michael, who was giving that calm and calculating gaze to her, but he rested his eyes on mine. She was a leggy young thing with long auburn hair and legs that didn't quit, and I was sure even if it wasn't for Michael's fortune, she'd be all over him just for his good looks too.

"So, there's something I've been meaning to ask you," I said to Michael.

"What is it?" He gave me his undivided attention, which made me smiled.

"How did you get into this whole…different lifestyle thing?"

Michael seemed amused at first but then he became serious. "Just a curiosity to explore the limits of my body, how far I was capable of going. I found it to be the ultimate test of what I can do and am capable of doing. That makes me feel quite aroused; knowing my power and that I can get people to do as I wish. It extends into all aspects of my life. This kind of sex, as you called 'alternative' I find fitting for the kind of personality I have. I like to explore my limits, and provide the ultimate pleasure for my lovers. And then again, maybe it's just because I love to fuck, and I have the need to fuck hard."

I nodded. It was true. Michael's money definitely got him things he wanted and pushed others to do what he wanted too. Sexually it was apparently the same thing. He'd already taken me further than I'd ever thought I'd go in the kinky parts of sex that I had shied away from previously. It was challenging, exhilarating, yet thrilling, always with a little bit of an element of danger.

"And the subs…how many have you had?"

"That's a bold question; one that I'd never tell, Fi. All you need to worry about and know is that you are my sub right now."

Rock Hard Love Hard (Rock Hard Musical #1)

"Did they quit or did you get bored with them?" I pressed on.

"A little of both, I guess."

"When was the last time you had one before me?"

"Are you sure you want to know that?"

"Yes, I'm sure," I replied.

"The first time we met at your graduate class while I was a guest lecturer, I had one. But as soon as I laid my eyes on you, and you came up to ask me a question after my lecture, I knew you were perfect for me. I had to have you, Fiona. You were so beautiful, so regal, yet sexy; I wanted to put my dick in you the moment you opened your mouth. But had to restrain myself. You were so innocent, so pure. I had to wait and go slow."

"You had quite the plan from the start, didn't you?"

Michael smiled. "You have been worth all the planning and waiting, Fi. You're that scrumptious and tantalizing."

"Oh," I said. He had been right when he cautioned me. I wasn't so sure I'd wanted to know what I had just been informed of; however, there would be no erasing it from my memory. It shouldn't bother me. It wasn't like I had never had a boyfriend in the past, but because of a painful past experience I had sexually with a man or rather a boy, I couldn't even think about being in a relationship with such explicit and demanding sex like what Michael longed for in a partner…play thing…whatever it was that I actually was.

An hour later, we had landed in Vegas and a limousine was waiting to take us to the hotel, which was the Hard Rock Hotel and Casino, right off the strip. It was an impressive hotel and I looked out the window at the reflection of the limousine against the doors that were its entrance. Someone was at the door right away, greeting

Mr. Bailey and smiling at me as I got out. There was no need to stand in line and check in. We didn't even have to go through the casino to get to the elevators that took us to our room. We went up a private elevator with its own operator, got on, and then shot right up to the top floor, where the doors opened and revealed an amazing penthouse suite.

"I figured a place devoted to rock stars and their wild ways was perfect for my little director of a rock musical…the one who is so eager to explore and prove that she is a worthy sub."

I nodded my head, biting down on my tongue. Had it really looked like I was trying to prove myself to be a worthy sub? I hadn't thought so, but apparently Michael had.

In the corner of the suite there was a large trunk on a stand. I looked at it curiously, knowing that it didn't fit in with the theme of the room. Michael saw me eyeing it up and took my hand, walking me over to it.

"Do you know what this is?" he asked.

"No," I replied.

"It's what's going to give us such a special weekend together," he replied. "I'll show you…it'll give you something to look forward to."

Michael opened up the trunk and began to show me what was in there and what I'd be partaking in over the next few days. Some devices were beyond what my creative imagination could even understand and others were the things you heard about more when it came to bondage and those sorts of things. There were nipple clamps, leather outfits, crops, various sized devices for various orifices, and an array of gels and creams, each that were designed to provide a different sensation or stimulation.

Rock Hard Love Hard (Rock Hard Musical #1)

"So, what do you think?" Michael asked.

"I'm not sure what to think," I said.

He smiled and reached for something in the chest. "Then we'll try this." He pulled out a long black silk scarf and began to tie it around my eyes.

"Don't move or do anything or you'll pay the price. I'm in charge. Do you understand?"

I breathed in, debating the situation. I knew Michael was into this and had let him slowly bring me to this point after having great vanilla sex before, but now faced with actually spending an entire weekend doing this, using all those strange objects on me, mostly, made me question what I really wanted. I was at a point where it was all or nothing. What did I really want? Was this something that I could do? It was Michael's thing, but that didn't mean it was mine.

"Stop," I said quietly. I turned around and made it so he couldn't fasten the blindfold. "I don't want this Michael. This isn't for me."

"You're just nervous," he said, trying to continue tying the blindfold.

"No, I'm not nervous. I am telling you that I don't want to do it."

"You are going to do this," he said. His chiseled jaw was tense and he was staring at me with sparking eyes. Part of him looked aroused by my defiance and that scared me.

"I've tried these things because they are important to you and I wanted to please you, but I just can't do it. I don't want to be with you if it's just about sex…especially this type of sex, Michael."

"What? We have an understanding, Fiona. When we began this, you knew what I wanted. Yes, I want you for sex. I want you because I desire you. We've got a good thing going and I call you girlfriend. You've met my parents, and I've done everything to try to please you. What more could you want? I've given you everything and this is all I ask for in return," he said, holding the scarf out in his clenched fist.

I took a deep breath. "I am grateful for everything you've done for me, Michael. I owe a lot to you, but if you want this type of sex for repayment, I'll have to find another way. I've enjoyed the kind we've had so far, but this… I'm sorry. It's time I stand on my own two feet and count on my skills to get me ahead in the world, not just the connections that come from being your current possession. I'll be eternally grateful for what you've done for me, but I want something more than this, this master-sub thing."

"You ingrate," Michael hissed. "Do you know how many women would do anything to be in the position you're in? You're going to throw it all away because you just aren't into this type of sex. You haven't even experienced it, how would you know you wouldn't like it? If you'd only trust me more, let me take you to your sexual height, I know you'd like it. Even if you didn't, it's a small price to pay for everything I have to offer you."

"Yeah, until you get sick of me. How long does that usually take?" I said. I was starting to get angry. I didn't want to fight, but I had a right to state what was acceptable to me and what wasn't, whether Michael liked it or not. I read somewhere in some book or so that even in this kind of sexual relationship, there are rules of acceptability from both parties for it to work. Since he wasn't following any rules it seemed, he could take his dominant nature and shove it up his ass if he felt differently.

Now I was getting mad. Before Michael could say another word, I said, "Michael, I won't be forced into anything I don't want to do. I'm going to be moving out and it was probably better that I did it immediately."

Rock Hard Love Hard (Rock Hard Musical #1)

"You're bluffing. Where would you go?" Michael asked, his face incredulous. He couldn't believe anyone would refuse him like this.

"I'm resourceful enough to find a place to crash until I get a job and my own place," I said. "Don't worry, I have means, too."

I began to get dressed and Michael came up to me and whipped me around, squeezing my arm tightly. "If this is because of Hay you'll both pay the price. Hay won't have this little career he's so gung ho to get and you'll find yourself facing considerably more obstacles to get your little musical out there."

I wrenched my arm out of his grip, and said calmly, "this has nothing to do with Hay. It has everything to do with me and if I have to start all over and face some obstacles I'll do it. I'm not afraid of hard work," I said. "Besides, I never asked you to help me on this musical. You were the one to suggest putting it on for real. You were the one who thought I had talent, took me under your wings, and wanted me to move in with you." I yanked my arm out of Michael's reach and turned away from him and started to get dressed again. However, I had to think carefully, I couldn't put Hay in such a position as that. I knew Michael would easily be able to make his life hell and that it would be my fault if I let that happen. No, I needed a clean break and a fresh start. It was something I needed to do on my own. Being dependent was never my true nature and it couldn't be if I really wanted to develop a reputation based on my own merits and abilities.

Michael walked around to me so he was looking at me. "Look, I'm sorry, Fiona. You are a very smart and intelligent woman, talented and beautiful. I wouldn't have supported you so much just to have sex with you. I wouldn't have arranged for you to live with me if all I desired from you was sex. I can't help but want you though. Very much. Constantly. Being with you has turned me upside down, and I can't help being what I am with you...a sexual beast. You bring out my desire to dominate you completely with my primal urges. Yet, I find your defiance more arousing. Come on, just stay and let's talk this through. I'll shut the trunk up and not mention it again until you're ready."

I smiled. "That's nice, Michael, but I don't think there is any point. You have said that it's a part of what you want in life and that's fine. Obviously many women like that sort of thing too. I'm just not one of them. This really is for the best. I can't be what you want me to be. I love being with you, but I can't go there. I don't think I ever will. I'm sorry you had to go through so much work to arrange for this weekend."

"So, you're really going?" Michael's face fell, and a look of desperation crossed his eyes.

I bit my lips and nodded before I could change my mind. "Please don't make this any harder than it is, Michael."

Michael looked down for a moment, before he looked up. He took a deep breath before saying, "Okay. Should I have the jet fly you back?"

"No, that's okay. I'll go to the airport and catch the first flight I can," I said.

"There's no need to get extreme, Fiona. Maybe I can fly back with you."

"No, stay, Michael. You wanted to come out to Vegas for a fun weekend. You should stay and have fun, but...not with me."

"Fiona..." Michael began. "I was hoping to spend the weekend with you. How could I even think of spending it here when..." his face fell.

"I'm sure you'll be able to find something to do, Michael," I said, zipping up my bag and toting it out of the room.

Rock Hard Love Hard (Rock Hard Musical #1)

Ten minutes later, I was boarding a taxi, making my way to the airport. It turned out that I had to wait for four hours for a flight, but I didn't mind. I sat at one of the noisy slot machines, plugging in quarters, and drank a cold beer. It was nice and relaxing. And completely contrary to what I would be doing with Michael all weekend.

As I prepared to hop on the plane that headed back to Los Angeles, I caught a glimpse of myself in the mirror. My eyes were shining, bright, clear, and full of hopes and dreams. I had just directed a smash musical, and despite how disappointed I was in ending my relationship with Michael, I also felt a kind of liberation, like a weight had been taken off my shoulders. I was not going to be anyone's submissive physically, emotionally, and psychologically. That was my limit.

Especially since I've spent years trying to forget what happened to me when I was a teen and how one of my swim coach tried to force himself on me, threatened to throw me off the team and get my swim scholarship revoked. I needed that scholarship to go to college, but it was a mistake to have to sell myself to get it. His dominance and demands on me were so horrific, I blocked it from my memories. Became frigid and sexually aversed for several years afterwards until I went to graduate school and had to explore all sides of me as a director. Then that's when I met Michael, who opened up that hidden side of me and pushed me there again.

He had helped me become more confident and adventurous, for sure, but he had also pushed me more than I could or would go again.

For a moment I grieved the ending of our relationship, but then perked up when I truly realized, it was for the best.

CHAPTER 19

I called up an old college friend and stayed with her a few days while I sorted some things out and arranged a budget, something I hadn't had to think about in about a half a year. Yes, it stung a little that I had to admit I'd grown more addicted to the lavish lifestyle that I'd been living with Michael, but it wasn't going to debilitate me. I'd learned a lesson and now I was set to move on.

In the next couple of days, I had found an apartment near USC where I was hired to teach musical theater as a guest lecturer. The job came just at the nick of time, and I couldn't have hoped for a better situation.

But then fate had a way of surprising us with more unexpected rewards when we have the right attitude and openness to what life had to offer when my phone went off, playing the lead song of Rock Hard Love Hard…The Beat of My Heart, which I had programmed in from the soundtrack.

"Hi Fiona," a familiar voice said. I couldn't have been more surprise to hear from this voice again especially how things had gone when we last saw each other. It had been only a few days since I left Michael, so I was shocked when Michael called me and asked me out on a date – just to talk.

I said yes, wondering if he'd perhaps decided to forget what happened that day in Vegas and was set to be friends.

The arrangement was to meet at a local steakhouse for a casual dinner. Michael had offered to pick me up, but I didn't want that. I didn't want to have any time alone with him where I might cross lines that made our relationship more confusing. So, I drove and met him there, wearing just a sundress, sandals, and light makeup.

Rock Hard Love Hard (Rock Hard Musical #1)

"You look lovely," Michael said, his eyes taking me in from head to toe. "Happy."

He looked terrible, as though he haven't slept or shaved for days.

"Thanks," I said. I laughed, knowing how different I must've looked to Michael since I wasn't dressed as eloquently as he was used to seeing me when we usually went out on the town dining, but I wanted it to be clear that I was there as a friend, not a sexual conquest.

"So, how have things been the past few days?"

"Really good, thanks. I've already settled into a cute apartment near USC, and guess what? I got the guest lecturer position in Musical Theater at USC. Thank you for putting in a good word for me."

"Can I be honest with you?" Michael asked, leaning forward so he was within inches of my face. "I didn't get a chance to even talk to the Musical Theater department about that. You got that job all on your own."

"Oh," I said, genuinely surprised, but thrilled. "I just thought…never mind."

Michael smiled a small smile and then reached over to hold my hands. "I'm so proud of you, but I'm here to also tell you that I miss you so badly," his voice broke. "It's only been a few days, but I can't stand it. Everything is different when you're not here. Everything at our place reminds me of you. My pillows smell of you. My shirts…the piano. I see the empty piano and keep expecting to hear your talented fingers fill our house with beautiful music."

Michael went on. "I'm lonely. I really had grown used to talking to you and living with someone. I can't stand not having that, Fiona. I want more. I want to work on having a real relationship with you, and know that it'll take a little effort on my part, but I'm willing to try. All I need is for you to say, 'yes, I'll give you a chance.' That'd make me one happy guy."

"I don't know Michael," I said. "I'm not so sure it's such a good idea. You have needs that…"

"Fiona, my only need is to have you in my life. That's what I'm focused on; that's what I'm passionate about. I didn't want to tell you before, I was afraid you'd leave me, but you did anyways…but what I feel for you…I love you. I didn't know that was what I was feeling, but I do. I just don't know how to show it."

"Oh Michael," I sighed, not sure what to say. "Dammit, I'm ready to move on, but seeing you again… I'm just nervous about it."

"How about some dates first? I won't ask you to commit to anything right away. Just give me a chance. Please."

I didn't know how it had happened, but I found myself saying that I would give Michael a chance, but only if it was different. I could never be a sub to his dom, and if he didn't understand that, then we would keep our relationship strictly platonic. Michael agreed, while looking genuinely happy.

"Thank you, Fiona," he said, reaching for my hands and bringing it up to his lips to kiss my knuckles before bringing them to his cheeks where he held them for a while. "I really do love you. I've always had," he said looking deep into my eyes. "Ever since you moved in with me, and I got to know you more than just a pretty face and sexy body."

Then as if we have never been apart, we lean in across the table and kissed, softly and then more passionately. Once his tongue entered my mouth and I had a taste of him, I couldn't stop kissing him. When we broke apart and I watched Michael go the opposite direction as I was heading for home, I couldn't help feel an ache for what we used to have, but also hopeful for what this new relationship could turn out to be. Michael had admitted he loved me, and that in itself, was considerable.

Despite us starting to 'date,' we managed to live in separate places. I had my apartment while he had his penthouse. When we saw each other while 'dating', our passion was heightened because of our separation, and things between us got even hotter than before.

One day, after my work-out, I got a call from Michael. "I have a fantastic idea. Do you have a minute?"

"Sure," I said. I got into her car, started it, and put him on the speaker. "What's up?"

"I have a brilliant idea."

"Yeah, what's that, Michael?"

"We need a break, a fun adventure for the two of us. What do you say to a summer in Europe? We could go to

Italy, Greece, Spain, and anywhere else you wanted to go. It would be wonderful, a real opportunity to grow even closer and enjoy an experience of a lifetime."

"I'm writing a new musical, Michael. I don't think I can spare the time off."

"You can write it during the trip. It would help inspire you."

I smiled. "That is a good point."

"Excellent. We'll go over the itinerary tonight. Whatever you want, I'm game for. You're the boss."

I started laughing, knowing that Michael was teasing me. I'd been very specific about not having those labels attached to our intimate moments and he'd really followed through on it, changing greatly. The result was explosive sex, more willingness to try things that I used to be afraid of, and a closer connection with Michael.

Rock Hard Love Hard (Rock Hard Musical #1)

Did I love Michael? Absolutely, but I wasn't sure if it was a love that would last. It really didn't matter at the moment though because it came at a perfect time.

EPILOGUE

Europe proved to be absolutely spectacular and really gave Michael and I a chance to grow as a couple, both deciding that we were meant to be in each other's lives and regardless of how freaked out either of us may be by that, we'd deal with the issues as they arose – that is, if they even arose.

"Good luck today, hon. You'll be the sexiest professor ever," Michael said.

"Thank you, sir. I wish you were my student. I'm actually really nervous. What if they don't think what I have to say is relevant?"

"Are you kidding? Ever since the musical, USC had considered you one of their royalty. You'll be great.

Rock Hard Love Hard (Rock Hard Musical #1)

That's why they called you when the position was opened and didn't even bother extending offers anywhere else."

"I still can't believe it," Fiona said. She stood up and took a sip of her coffee. "So, how do I look?"

"Sexy," Michael growled. "You will always look incredibly hot to me, babe."

"I was hoping for professional," I said laughing.

"Professional, yes, but a sexy professional," Michael countered laughing.

"Well, wish me luck," I said.

"Break a leg, hon."

"In these heels, that just might happen."

"They look good though," Michael replied. "I can't wait to take them off of you."

I smiled, staring back at Michael one more time. He'd changed so much and really had opened up, showing he was committed to seeing of our relationship had a chance. The time in Europe cemented that. We'd been very compatible and it was the most time we'd spent with each other consecutively since knowing each other.

A half hour later, I was walking into my new classroom, ready to teach my class in Dramatic Presentation to those who were first years in the drama program at USC.

Seeing all the eager faces excited me and I could recall when I was a student in that exact spot, ready to conquer the world in the theater, on screen, and anywhere else I could find.

About ten minutes into my lecture I got the flow of things and found myself in a groove. The kid who'd arrived late didn't even distract me. He was certainly someone who probably would never make it; arriving late to class, dressed with a hoodie tight around his head, and sitting way in the back. Why bother showing up? Annoyed, I decided then that I'd talk to him after class and set the tone.

Forty minutes later, and my first class was done. I breathed a sigh of relief. I felt good that it had been a success, but it was time to go tend to the part of my job that was not as exciting – being a disciplinarian when necessary. My natural instincts said that I just should ignore people who weren't serious about the class, but I knew that wasn't really the answer. It was the easy way out and I didn't want to get that rep as being a teacher that students wanted to take because she didn't care. I cared a great deal.

The students were filing out, some coming up and asking questions as they did so. The guy in the hoodie remained in the back of the classroom. *He probably fell asleep*, I thought. *Wait…should I be offended by that if he did?*

I walked up to the student and said, "Excuse me."

He looked up at me, and my breath caught in my throat at the intense blue eyes staring back at me. "Yes."

I just about toppled over. It was Hay.

His blue eyes took me all in, like he was appreciating something he hungered for.

I could hardly believe it. I haven't seen him for nearly four months and now there he was in my class. It made sense since he'd said he switched to drama, but I'd honestly not thought about it all summer with Michael spending so much time with me, visiting various theaters and opera houses across Europe.

Although I haven't thought of Hay as much throughout the summer, thinking there wasn't going to be any chance of us getting together; again, there was that instant heart-stopping gut reaction of pure lust and desire I had when I was around him. Even now, when he was no longer playing Tristan, he had that cocky swagger, that drop-dead gorgeous beauty that was rock star material.

"Hay, oh my God, how are you?"

"Great teacher. How about you?"

"Really good," I said.

"I'm sorry I was late. I was auditioning for a musical in New York and got here as quick as I could. The red eye was running late and it wasn't easy."

"Why'd you keep your hoodie up?"

"I wasn't sure if it'd disrupt your flow. I didn't want that to happen."

"That's very considerate because it likely would have. So, what have you been up to? Did you get the part?"

"I don't know yet, but it went well."

"Same agent?"

"No, that guy ended up being bogus. Canned me after the Vegas thing. It took me until last month to find another one. This one is considerably better though, lots of leads at places that seem to actually make sense – not the middle of the desert," he said laughing.

"Well, that's great. You look real good," I said, taking him all in with my eyes...his muscular arms and biceps clearly showed through his sweatshirt, as his thick rock hard abs. I knew he was probably wearing no t-shirt under his sweatshirt. "Your injuries completely healed now?" I asked. "Any chance of you going back to play football?"

Rock Hard Love Hard (Rock Hard Musical #1)

Hay shook his head. "Coach is working me in slowly, but I missed a lot of time. I started training again just to get ready and in shape." He playfully flexed his bicep, and I could see they were more defined than before. Then he lifted his sweatshirt, showing me his ribs where he had really messed up his body before, and aside from a healing scar line, it was ripped, sexy, and hard. Looking at his naked torso brought back the memory of him being fully naked in my office that first day of rehearsals, and my face flushed as I remembered how much I wanted to feel him against me and in me. I swallowed as Hay's eyes suddenly flicker at me as though he was thinking the same thing. "Um, I guess I'd better get going. I don't have another class for a bit," I said quickly, licking my lips.

I reached out and gave Hay a hug and began to walk away. Every one of my nerves was on fire, shocked by the sudden appearance of Hay in my classroom and my body's primal response to him. I thought it would be gone by now, but it's stronger than before, and he looked so much sexier than before.

"Wait!" Hay shouted.

"Yes," I said.

He got up and ran towards me, pinning me against the classroom door before his mouth crashed into mine kissing me passionately and wildly, not willing to stop unless I stopped him. I moaned, throwing my head back, not able to stop him.

This is what I've been waiting for all this time.

I let Hay devour my mouth and kiss every inch of me with his lips, making me burn with his every touch. His hands traveled all over my body, tweaking, teasing, rubbing me in all my zones that had me pressing up to him, wanting more of him everywhere. As much as I tried, I couldn't resist their touch. I have been craving him since the first day I've seen him.

Rock Hard Love Hard (Rock Hard Musical #1)

Hay's hands made their way down to my skirt and he slowly lifted it up, gliding his hands up as he slid my panties to the side, entering me with three of his fingers, and making me gasp. I was so wet, his fingers slid in and out easily, as he pressed his hard-on against me. "I haven't stopped thinking about you, Fiona," Hay said through a husky whisper. "Or wanting you," he said, as he dipped his face down to nuzzle at my nipple.

I moaned, feeling how badly he wanted me. I reached out my hands and touched his bare chest, savoring the smooth feel of him against my hand. He groaned, as I slowly flicked his nipple, and then everything exploded as we suddenly couldn't get enough of each other, using everything we've got to explore each other's bodies and slid our hands up and down them, wanting to memorize every detail of each other.

I reached down and unzipped Hay's pants to free his aching hard-on. With a groan, he easily slid into me, gently moving up and down inside me with my back pressed against the door and one of my legs now up on the chair by the exit.

"Oh. My. God, Fiona!" Hay groaned into my face. "This is everything I've dreamed about and more. I..." he didn't finish his sentence as he began pumping more furiously, harder, louder.

I gasped and moaned, taking it all in and savoring the experience that I'd denied myself several times in the past. A voice in the back of my mind was telling me I should say no, but I couldn't. All that came out of my mouth was, "yes, yes."

I couldn't stop myself and suddenly my body tensed so tightly before I came hard, followed by Hay. He was breathing heavy, but the words he whispered in my ear were very clear. "I'm not letting you go, Fiona. If you won't leave Michael then I will be content with taking what I can have of you, by becoming your lover. I've tried to get you out of my mind for nearly half a year. I've tried everything, even purposely avoiding you for months, and even trying to see other women while we were rehearsing the musical. But you're like an itch I can't get rid of. A very sexy and amazing itch I don't want to lose. There's a reason you're in there and I'm not going to avoid it any longer. I fucking love you." His hand caressed my face and his eyes bore into mine. "Some day you'll leave him and see he's not the right one for you and I'll be there, ready to give you all of me, not just a selective little bit."

"Hay, I…" I began.

He pressed his finger on my lips. "Don't say a word."

Then he zipped up his pants, while I adjusted my clothes. I was flushed and couldn't hide that I had loved every bit of what I've just experienced. Hay turned to me and smiled. "I'll see you tomorrow, teacher."

I could hardly breathe. Hay? Michael? Suddenly everything became much more complicated.

Kailin Gow

*****

Hay, Fiona, and Michael will be back in Book 2 of Rock Hard Musical.

Rock Hard Fight Hard (Rock Hard Musical #2)

Visit theEDGEbooks.com to sign up for when Book 2 will be released.

About Kailin Gow

Kailin Gow was a peer counselor at the Women's Center during her undergraduate years. She produced and hosted a women's issues radio show and ran workshops and seminars in the community for women covering women's issues including self-esteem, sexuality, identity, and gender roles. She was an intern at Juvenile Court, working for the public defenders with teen charges. As an undergraduate at UC Irvine, she was also teacher's assistant in Criminology and Constitutional Law.

Never thinking she would be interested in the topic, she took her human sexuality class in college, and aced it, being voted by her group as the girl most of the classmates wanted to be stranded with on an island. She'd like to think it was because she knew so much about the subject, of course, not just because the college class was made up of mostly men.

Kailin Gow today is the author of several books for women, New Adults, and Young Adults. She divides her time living in the OC, Las Vegas, Dallas, and London, England with her Alpha husband and her Bad Ass in Training little girl.

Sign Up for Kailin Gow's New Adult and Adult Only (18 and up) Newsletter

where she will have excerpts from new books, tips on intimacy, dating and relationships, empowering quotes for women and men, sexual tips, news on new releases and more.

http://www.KailinGowBooks.com

Subject line: Kailin Gow's New Adult and Adult Only Newsletter